NaaC

D1552649

WORKING FOR BIGFOOT

Stories from the Dresden Files

WORKING FOR BIGFOOT

Stories from the Dresden Files

Jim Butcher

Subterranean Press 2015

First Edition

ISBN
978-1-59606-730-1

Copyright information for individual stories is on page 131.

Subterranean Press
PO Box 190106
Burton, MI 48519

subterraneanpress.com

Table of Contents

B Is for Bigfoot

Takes place between *Fool Moon* and *Grave Peril*

When people come to the only professional wizard in the Chicago phone book for help, they're one of two things: desperate or smart. Very rarely are they both.

The smart ones come to me because they know I can help—the desperate because they don't know anyone else who can. With a smart client, the meeting is brief and pleasant. Someone has lost the engagement ring that was a family heirloom, and has been told I'm a man who can find lost things. Such people engage my services (preferably in cash), I do the job, and everyone's happy.

Desperate clients, on the other hand, can pull all sorts of ridiculous nonsense. They lie to me about what kind of trouble they've gotten themselves into, or try to pass me a check I'm sure will bounce like a basketball. Occasionally they demand that I prove my powers by telling them what their problem is before they even shake my hand—in which case, the problem is that they're idiots.

My newest client wanted something different, though. He wanted me to meet him in the woods.

This did not make me feel optimistic that he would be one of the smart ones.

Woods being in short supply in Chicago, I had to drive all the way up to the northern half of Wisconsin to get to decent timber. That took me about six hours, given that my car, while valiant and bold, is also a Volkswagen Beetle made around the same time flower children were big. By the time I got there and had hiked a mile or two out into the woods, to the appointed location, dark was coming on.

I'm not a moron, usually. I've made enemies during my stint as a professional wizard. So when I settled down to wait for the client, I did so with my staff in one hand, my blasting rod in the other, and a .38 revolver in the pocket of my black leather duster. I blew out a small crater in the earth with an effort of will, using my staff to direct the energy, and built a modest campfire in it.

Then I stepped out of the light of the campfire, found a comfortable, shadowy spot, and waited to see who was going to show up.

The whole PI gig is mostly about patience. You have to talk to a lot of people who don't know anything to find the one who does. You have to sit around waiting a lot, watching for someone to do something before you catch them doing it. You have to do a lot of searching through useless information to get to one piece of really good information. Impatient PIs rarely conclude an investigation successfully, and never remain in the business for long. So when an hour went by without anything happening, I wasn't too worried.

By two hours, though, my legs were cramping and I had a little bit of a headache, and apparently the mosquitoes had decided to hold a convention about ten feet away because I was covered with bites. Given that I hadn't been paid a dime yet, this client was getting annoying, fast.

The fire had died down to almost nothing, so I almost didn't see the creature emerge from the forest and crouch down beside the embers.

The thing was huge. I mean, just saying that it was nine feet tall wasn't enough. It was mostly human-shaped, but it was built more heavily than any human, covered in layers and layers of ropy muscle that were visible even through a layer of long, dark brown hair or fur that covered its whole body. It had a brow ridge like a mountain crag, with dark, glittering eyes that reflected the red-orange light of the fire.

I did not move. Not even a little. If that thing wanted to hurt me, I would have one hell of a time stopping it from doing so, even with magic, and unless I got lucky, something with that much mass would find my .38 about as deadly as a pricing gun.

Then it turned its head and part of its upper body toward me and said, in a rich, mellifluous Native American accent, "You done over there? Don't mean to be rude, and I didn't want to interrupt you, wizard, but there's business to be done."

My jaw dropped open. I mean it literally dropped open.

I stood up slowly, and my muscles twitched and ached. It's hard to stretch out a cramp while you remain in a stance, prepared to run away at an instant's notice, but I tried.

"You're…," I said. "You're a…"

"Bigfoot," he said. "Sasquatch. Yowie. Yeti. Buncha names. Yep."

"And you…you called me?" I felt a little stunned. "Um…did you use a pay phone?"

I instantly imagined him trying to punch little phone buttons with those huge fingers. No, of course he hadn't done that.

"Nah," he said, and waved a huge, hairy arm to the north. "Fellas at the reservation help us make calls sometimes. They're a good bunch."

I shook myself and took a deep breath. For Pete's sake, I was a wizard. I dealt with the supernatural all the time. I shouldn't be this rattled by one little unexpected encounter. I shoved my nerves and my discomfort down and replaced them with iron professionalism—or at least the semblance of calm.

I emerged from my hidey-hole and went over to the fire. I settled down across from the Bigfoot, noting as I did that I was uncomfortably close to being within reach of his long arms. "Um...welcome. I'm Harry Dresden."

The Bigfoot nodded and looked at me expectantly. After a moment of that, he said, as if prompting a child, "This is your fire."

I blinked. Honoring the obligations of hospitality is a huge factor in the supernatural communities around the world—and as it was my campfire, I was the de facto host, and the Bigfoot my guest. I said, "Yes. I'll be right back."

I hurried back to my car and came back to the campfire with two cans of warm Coke and half a tin of salt-and-vinegar Pringles chips. I opened both cans and offered the Bigfoot one of them. Then I opened the Pringles and divided them into two stacks, offering him his choice of either.

The Bigfoot accepted them and sipped almost delicately at the Coke, handling the comparatively tiny can with far more grace than I would have believed. The chips didn't get the careful treatment. He popped them all into his mouth and chomped down on them enthusiastically. I emulated him. I got a lot of crumbs on the front of my coat.

The Bigfoot nodded at me. "Hey, got any smokes?"

"No," I said. "Sorry. It's not a habit."

"Maybe next time," he said. "Now. You have given me your name, but I have not given you mine. I am called Strength of a River in His Shoulders, of the Three Stars Forest People. And there is a problem with my son."

"What kind of problem?" I asked.

"His mother can tell you in greater detail than I can," River Shoulders said.

"His mother?" I rubbernecked. "Is she around?"

"No," he said. "She lives in Chicago."

I blinked. "His mother…"

"Human," River Shoulders said. "The heart wants what the heart wants, yeah?"

Then I got it. "Oh. He's a scion."

That made more sense. A lot of supernatural folk can and do interbreed with humanity. The resulting children, half mortal, half supernatural, are called scions. Being a scion means different things to different children, depending on their parentage, but they rarely have an easy time of it in life.

River Shoulders nodded. "Forgive my ignorance of the issues. Your society is…not one of my areas of expertise."

I know, right? A Bigfoot saying "expertise."

I shook my head a little. "If you can't tell me anything, why did you call me here? You could have told me all of this on the phone."

"Because I wanted you to know that I thought the problem supernatural in origin, and that I would have good reason to recognize it. And because I brought your retainer." He rummaged in a buckskin pouch that he wore slung across the front of his body. It had been all but invisible amid his thick pelt. He reached a hand in and tossed something at me.

I caught it on reflex and nearly yelped as it hit my hand. It was the size of a golf ball and extraordinarily heavy. I held it closer to the fire and then whistled in surprise.

Gold. I was holding a nugget of pure gold. It must have been worth…uh…well, a *lot.*

"We knew all the good spots a long time before the Europeans came across the sea," River Shoulders said calmly. "There's another, just as large, when the work is done."

"What if I don't take your case?" I asked him.

He shrugged. "I try to find someone else. But word is that you can be trusted. I would prefer you."

I regarded River Shoulders for a moment. He wasn't trying to intimidate me. It was a mark in his favor, because it wouldn't have been difficult. In fact, I realized, he was going out of his way to avoid that very thing.

"He's your son," I asked. "Why don't you help him?"

He gestured at himself and smiled slightly. "Maybe I would stand out a little in Chicago."

I snorted and nodded. "Maybe you would."

"So, wizard," River Shoulders asked. "Will you help my son?"

I pocketed the gold nugget and said, "One of these is enough. And yes. I will."

The next day I went to see the boy's mother at a coffee shop on the north side of town.

Dr. Helena Pounder was an impressive woman. She stood maybe six-four, and looked as though she might be able to bench-press more than I could. She wasn't really pretty, but her square, open face looked honest, and her eyes were a sparkling shade of springtime green.

When I came in, she rose to greet me and shook my hand. Her hands were an odd mix of soft skin and calluses—whatever she did for a living, she did it with tools in her hand.

"River told me he'd hired you," Dr. Pounder said. She gestured for me to sit, and we did.

"Yeah," I said. "He's a persuasive guy."

Pounder let out a rueful chuckle and her eyes gleamed. "I suppose he is."

"Look," I said. "I don't want to get too personal, but..."

"But how did I hook up with a Bigfoot?" she asked.

I shrugged and tried to look pleasant.

"I was at a dig site in Ontario—I'm an archaeologist—and I stayed a little too long in the autumn. The snows caught me there, a series of storms that lasted for more than a month. No one could get in to rescue me, and I couldn't even call out on the radio to let them know I was still at the site." She shook her head. "I fell sick and had no food. I might have died if someone hadn't started leaving rabbits and fish in the night."

I smiled. "River Shoulders?"

She nodded. "I started watching, every night. One night the storm cleared up at just the right moment, and I saw him there." She shrugged. "We started talking. Things sort of went from there."

"So the two of you aren't actually married, or...?"

"Why does that matter?" she asked.

I spread my hands in an apologetic gesture. "He paid me. You didn't. It might have an effect on my decision process."

"Honest enough, aren't you?" Pounder said. She eyed me for a moment and then nodded in something like approval. "We aren't married. But suitors aren't exactly knocking down my door—and I never saw much use for a husband anyway. River and I are comfortable with things as they are."

"Good for you," I said. "Tell me about your son."

She reached into a messenger bag that hung on the back of her diner chair and passed me a five-by-seven photograph of a kid, maybe eight or nine years old. He wasn't pretty, either, but his features had a kind of juvenile appeal, and his grin was as real and warm as sunlight.

"His name is Irwin," Pounder said, smiling down at the picture. "My angel."

Even tough, bouncer-looking supermoms have a soft spot for their kids, I guess. I nodded. "What seems to be the problem?"

"Earlier this year," she said, "he started coming home with injuries. Nothing serious—abrasions and bruises and scratches. But I suspect that the injuries were likely worse before the boy came home. Irwin heals very rapidly, and he's never been sick: literally never, not a day in his life."

"You think someone is abusing him," I said. "What did he say about it?"

"He made excuses," Pounder said. "They were obviously fictions, but that boy is at least as stubborn as his father, and he wouldn't tell me where or how he'd been hurt."

"Ah," I said.

She frowned. "Ah?"

"It's another kid."

Pounder blinked. "How..."

"I have the advantage over you and your husband, inasmuch as I have actually been a grade-school boy before," I said. "If he snitches about it to the teachers or to you, he'll probably have to deal with retributive friction from his classmates. He won't be cool. He'll be a snitching, tattling pariah."

Pounder sat back in her seat, frowning. "I'm...hardly a master of social skills. I hadn't thought of it that way."

I shrugged. "On the other hand, you clearly aren't the sort to sit around wringing her hands, either."

Pounder snorted and gave me a brief, real smile.

"So," I went on, "when he started coming home hurt, what did you do about it?"

"I started escorting him to school and picking him up the moment class let out. That's been for the past two months—he hasn't had any more injuries. But I have to go to a conference tomorrow morning and—"

"You want someone to keep an eye on him."

"That, yes," she said. "But I also want you to find out who has been trying to hurt him."

I arched an eyebrow. "How am I supposed to do that?"

"I used River's financial advisor to pull some strings. You're expected to arrive at the school tomorrow morning to begin work as the school janitor."

I blinked. "Wait. Bigfoot has a financial advisor? *Who?* Like, Nessie?"

"Don't be a child," she said. "The human tribes assist the Forest People by providing an interface. River's folk give financial, medical, and educational aid in return. It works."

My imagination provided me with an image of River Shoulders standing in front of a children's music class, his huge fingers waving a baton that had been reduced to a matchstick by his enormity.

Sometimes my head is like an Etch A Sketch. I shook it a little, and the image went away.

"Right," I said. "It might be difficult to get you something actionable."

Pounder's eyes almost seemed to turn a green-tinged shade of gold, and her voice became quiet and hard. "I am not interested in courts," she said. "I only care about my son."

Yikes.

Bigfoot Irwin had himself one formidable mama bear. If it turned out that I was right and he was having issues with another child, that could cause problems. People can overreact to things when their kids get involved. I might have to be careful with how much truth got doled out to Dr. Pounder.

Nothing's ever simple, is it?

The school was called the Madison Academy, and it was a private elementary and middle school on the north side of town. Whatever strings River Shoulders had pulled, they were good ones. I ambled in the next morning, went into the administrative office, and was greeted with the enthusiasm of a cloister of diabetics meeting their insulin delivery truck. Their sanitation engineer had abruptly departed for a Hawaiian vacation, and they needed a temporary replacement.

So I wound up wearing a pair of coveralls that were too short in the arms, too short in the legs, and too short in the crotch, with the name "Norm" stenciled on the left breast. I was shown to my office, which was a closet with a tiny desk and several shelves stacked with cleaning supplies of the usual sort.

It could have been worse. The stencil could have read "Freddie."

So I started engineering sanitation. One kid threw up, and another started a paint fight with his friend in the art room. The office paged me on an old intercom system that ran throughout the halls and had an outlet in the closet when they needed something in particular, but by ten I was clear of the child-created havoc and dealing with the standard human havoc, emptying trash cans, sweeping floors and halls, and generally cleaning up. As I did, going from classroom to classroom to take care of any full trash cans, I kept an eye out for Bigfoot Irwin.

I spotted him by lunchtime, and I took my meal at a table set aside for faculty and staff in one corner of the cafeteria as the kids ate.

Bigfoot Irwin was one of the tallest boys in sight, and he hadn't even hit puberty yet. He was all skin and bones—and I recognized something else about him at once. He was a loner.

He didn't look like an unpleasant kid or anything, but he carried himself in a fashion that suggested that he was apart from the other children; not aloof, simply separate. His expression was distracted, and his mind was clearly a million miles away. He had a double-sized lunch and a paperback book crowding his tray, and he headed for one end of a lunch table. He sat down, opened the book with one hand, and started eating with the other, reading as he went.

The trouble seemed obvious. A group of five or six boys occupied the other end of his lunch table, and they leaned their heads closer together and started muttering to one another and casting covert glances at Irwin.

I winced. I knew where this was going. I'd seen it before, when it had been me with the book and the lunch tray.

Two of the boys stood up, and they looked enough alike to make me think that they either had been born very close together or else were fraternal twins. They both had messy, sandy brown hair, long, narrow faces, and pointed chins. They looked like they might have been a year or two ahead of Irwin, though they were both shorter than the lanky boy.

They split, moving down either side of the table toward Irwin, their footsteps silent. I hunched my shoulders and watched them out of the corner of my eye. Whatever they were up to, it wouldn't be lethal, not right here in front of half the school, and it might be possible to learn something about the pair by watching them in action.

They moved together, though not perfectly in synch. It reminded me of a movie I'd seen in high school about juvenile lions learning to hunt together. One of the kids, wearing a black baseball cap, leaned over the table and casually swatted the book out of Irwin's hands. Irwin started and turned toward him, lifting his hands into a vague, confused-looking defensive posture.

As he did, the second kid, in a red sweatshirt, casually drove a finger down onto the edge of Irwin's dining tray. It flipped up, spilling food and drink all over Irwin.

A bowl broke, silverware rattled, and the whole tray clattered down. Irwin sat there looking stunned while the two bullies cruised right on by, as casual as can be. They were already fifteen feet away when the other children in the dining hall had zeroed in on the sound and reacted to the mess with a round of applause and catcalls.

"Pounder!" snarled a voice, and I looked up to see a man in a white visor, sweatpants, and a T-shirt come marching in from the hallway outside the cafeteria. "Pounder, what is this mess?"

Irwin blinked owlishly at the barrel-chested man and shook his head. "I..." He glanced after the two retreating bullies and then around the cafeteria. "I guess...I accidentally knocked my tray over, Coach Pete."

Coach Pete scowled and folded his arms. "If this was the first time this had happened, I wouldn't think anything of it. But how many times has your tray ended up on the floor, Pounder?"

Irwin looked down. "This would be five, sir."

"Yes it would," said Coach Pete. He picked up the paperback Irwin had been reading. "If your head wasn't in these trashy science fiction books all the time, maybe you'd be able to feed yourself without making a mess."

"Yes, sir," Irwin said.

"*Hitchhiker's Guide to the Galaxy,*" Coach Pete said, looking at the book. "That's stupid. You can't hitchhike onto a spaceship."

"No, sir," Irwin said.

"Detention," Coach Pete said. "Report to me after school."

"Yes, sir."

Coach Pete slapped the paperback against his leg, scowled at Irwin—and then abruptly looked up at me. "What?" he demanded.

"I was just wondering. You don't, by any chance, have a Vogon in your family tree?"

Coach Pete eyed me, his chest swelling in what an anthropologist might call a threat display. It might have been impressive if I hadn't been talking to River Shoulders the night before. "That a joke?"

"That depends on how much poetry you write," I said.

At this Coach Pete looked confused. He clearly didn't like feeling that way, which seemed a shame, since I suspected he spent a lot of time doing it. Irwin's eyes widened and he darted a quick look at me. His mouth twitched, but the kid kept himself from smiling or laughing—which was fairly impressive in a boy his age.

Coach Pete glowered at me, pointed a finger as if it might have been a gun, and said, "You tend to your own business."

I held up both hands in a gesture of mild acceptance. I rolled my eyes as soon as Coach Pete turned his back, drawing another quiver of restraint from Irwin.

"Pick this up," Coach Pete said to Irwin, and gestured at the spilled lunch on the floor. Then he turned and stomped away, taking Irwin's paperback with him. The two kids who had been giving Irwin grief had made their way back to their original seats, meanwhile, and were at the far end of the table, looking smug.

I pushed my lunch away and got up from the table. I went over to Irwin's side and knelt down to help him clean up his mess. I picked up the tray, slid it to a point between us, and said, "Just stack it up here."

Irwin gave me a quick, shy glance from beneath his mussed hair, and started plucking up fallen bits of lunch. His hands were almost comically large compared to the rest of him, but his fingers were quick and dexterous. After a few seconds he asked, "You've read the *Hitchhiker's Guide*?"

"Forty-two times," I said.

He smiled and then ducked his head again. "No one else here likes it."

"Well, it's not for everyone, is it?" I asked. "Personally, I've always wondered if Adams might not be a front man for a particularly talented dolphin. Which I think would make the book loads funnier."

Irwin let out a quick bark of laughter and then hunched his shoulders and kept cleaning up. His shoulders shook.

"Those two boys give you trouble a lot?" I asked.

Irwin's hands stopped moving for a second. Then he started up again. "What do you mean?"

"I mean I've been you before," I said. "The kid who liked reading books about aliens and goblins and knights and explorers at lunch, and in class, and during recess. I didn't care much about sports. And I got picked on a lot."

"They don't pick on me," Irwin said quickly. "It's just...just what guys do. They give me a hard time. It's in fun."

"And it doesn't make you angry," I said. "Not even a little."

His hands slowed down, and his face turned thoughtful. "Sometimes," he said quietly. "When they spoil my broccoli."

I blinked. "Broccoli?"

"I love broccoli," Irwin said, looking up at me, his expression serious.

"Kid," I said, smiling, "no one loves broccoli. No one even *likes* broccoli. All the grown-ups just agree to lie about it so that we can make kids eat it, in vengeance for what our parents did to us."

"Well, I love broccoli," Irwin said, his jaw set.

"Hunh," I said. "Guess I've seen something new today." We finished and I said, "Go get some more lunch. I'll take care of this."

"Thank you," he said soberly. "Um, Norm."

I grunted, nodded to him, tossed the dropped food, and returned the tray. Then I sat back down at the corner table with my lunch and watched Irwin and his tormentors from the corner of my eye. The two bullies never took their eyes off Irwin, even while talking and joking with their group.

I recognized that behavior, though I'd never seen it in a child before; only in hunting cats, vampires, and sundry monsters.

The two kids were predators.

Young and inexperienced, maybe. But predators.

For the first time, I thought that Bigfoot Irwin might be in real trouble.

I went back to my own tray and wolfed down the "food" on it. I wanted to keep a closer eye on Irwin.

Being a wizard is all about being prepared. Well, that and magic, obviously. While I could do a few things in a hurry, most magic takes long moments or hours to arrange, and that means you have to know what's coming. I'd brought a few things with me, but I needed more information before I could act decisively on the kid's behalf.

I kept track of Irwin after he left the cafeteria. It wasn't hard. His face was down, his eyes on his book, and even though he was one of the younger kids in the school, he stood out, tall and gangly. I contrived to go past his classroom several times in the next hour. It was trig, which I knew, except I'd been doing it in high school.

Irwin was the youngest kid in the class. He was also evi-
dently the smartest. He never looked up from his book. Several
times the teacher tried to catch him out, asking him questions.
Irwin put his finger on the place in his book, glanced up at the
blackboard, and answered them with barely a pause. I found
myself grinning.

Next I tracked down Irwin's tormentors. They weren't hard
to find, either, since they both sat in the chairs closest to the
exit, as though they couldn't wait to go off and be delinquent the
instant school was out. They sat in class with impatient, sullen
expressions. They looked like they were in the grip of agoniz-
ing boredom, but they didn't seem to be preparing to murder a
teacher or anything.

I had a hunch that something about Irwin was drawing a
predatory reaction from those two kids. And Coach Vogon had
arrived on the scene pretty damned quickly—too much so for
coincidence, maybe.

"Maybe Bigfoot Irwin isn't the only scion at this school," I
muttered to myself.

And maybe I wasn't the only one looking out for the interests
of a child born with one foot in this world and one in another.

I was standing outside the gymnasium as the last class of
the day let out, leaning against the wall on my elbows, my feet
crossed at the heels, my head hanging down, my wheeled bucket
and mop standing unused a good seven feet away—pretty much
the picture of an industrious janitor. The kids went hurrying by
in a rowdy herd, with Irwin's tormentors being the last to leave
the gym. I felt their eyes on me as they went past, but I didn't
react to them.

Coach Vogon came out last, flicking out the banks of fluorescent lights as he went, his footsteps brisk and heavy. He came to a dead stop as he came out of the door and found me waiting for him.

There was a long moment of silence while he sized me up. I let him. I wasn't looking for a fight, and I had taken the deliberately relaxed and nonconfrontational stance I was in to convey that concept to him. I figured he was connected to the supernatural world, but I didn't know *how* connected he might be. Hell, I didn't even know if he was human.

Yet.

"Don't you have work to do?" he demanded.

"Doing it," I said. "I mean, obviously."

I couldn't actually hear his eyes narrow, but I was pretty sure they did. "You got a lot of nerve, buddy, talking to an instructor like that."

"If there weren't all these kids around, I might have said another syllable or two," I drawled. "Coach Vogon."

"You're about to lose your job, buddy. Get to work or I'll report you for malingering."

"Malingering," I said. "Four whole syllables. You're good."

He rolled another step toward me and jabbed a finger into my chest. "Buddy, you're about to buy a lot of trouble. Who do you think you are?"

"Harry Dresden," I said. "Wizard."

And I looked at him as I opened my Sight.

A wizard's Sight is an extra sense, one that allows him to perceive the patterns of energy and magic that suffuse the universe—energy that includes every conceivable form of magic. It doesn't actually open a third eye in your forehead or anything, but the brain translates the perceptions into the visual spectrum. In the circles I run in, the Sight shows you things as they truly are, cutting through every known form of veiling magic, illusion, and other mystic chicanery.

In this case, it showed me that the thing standing in front of me wasn't human.

Beneath its illusion, the spindly humanoid creature stood a little more than five feet high, and it might have weighed a hundred pounds soaking wet. It was naked, and anatomically it resembled a Ken doll. Its skin was a dark grey, its eyes absolutely huge, bulbous, and midnight black. It had a rounded, high-crowned head and long, delicately pointed ears. I could still see the illusion of Coach Pete around the creature, a vague and hazy outline.

It lowered the lids of its bulbous eyes, the gesture somehow exceptionally lazy, and then nodded slowly. It inclined its head the smallest measurable amount possible and murmured, in a melodious and surprisingly deep voice, "Wizard."

I blinked a few times and waved my Sight away, so that I was facing Coach Pete again. "We should talk," I said.

The apparent man stared at me unblinkingly, his expression as blank as a discarded puppet's. It was probably my imagination that made his eyes look suddenly darker. "Regarding?"

"Irwin Pounder," I said. "I would prefer to avoid a conflict with Svartalfheim."

He inhaled and exhaled slowly through his nose. "You recognized me."

In fact, I'd been making an educated guess, but the svartalf didn't need to know that. I knew precious little about the creatures. They were extremely gifted craftsmen, and were responsible for creating most of the really cool artifacts of Norse myth. They weren't wicked, exactly, but they were ruthless, proud, stubborn, and greedy, which often added up to similar results. They were known to be sticklers for keeping their word,

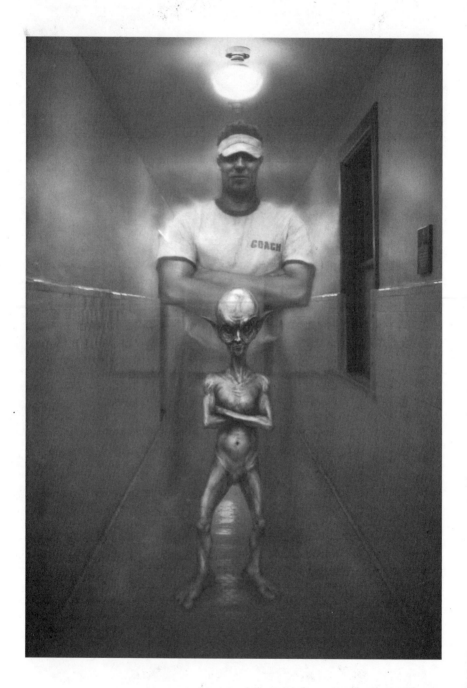

and God help you if you broke yours to them. Most important, they were a small supernatural nation unto themselves: one that protected its citizens with maniacal zeal.

"I had a good teacher," I said. "I want your boys to lay off Irwin Pounder."

"Point of order," he said. "They are not mine. I am not their progenitor. I am a guardian only."

"Be that as it may," I said, "my concern is for Irwin, not the brothers."

"He is a whetstone," he said. "They sharpen their instincts upon him. He is good for them."

"They aren't good for him," I said. "Fix it."

"It is not my place to interfere with them," Coach Pete said. "Only to offer indirect guidance and to protect them from anyone who would interfere with their growth."

The last phrase was as emotionless as the first, but it somehow carried an ugly ring of a threat—a polite threat, but a threat nonetheless.

Sometimes I react badly to being threatened. I might have glared a little.

"Hypothetically," I said, "let's suppose that I saw those boys giving Irwin a hard time again, and I made it my business to stop them. What would you do?"

"Slay you," Coach Pete said. His tone was utterly absent of any doubt.

"Awfully sure of yourself, aren't you."

He spoke as if reciting a single-digit arithmetic problem. "You are young. I am not."

I felt my jaw clench, and forced myself to take a slow breath, to stay calm. "They're hurting him."

"Be that as it may," he said calmly, "my concern is for the brothers, not for Irwin Pounder."

I ground my teeth and wished I could pick my words out of them before continuing the conversation. "We've both stated our positions," I said. "How do we resolve the conflict?"

"That also is not my concern," he said. "I will not dissuade the brothers. I will slay you should you attempt to do so yourself. There is nothing else to discuss."

He shivered a little, and suddenly the illusion of Coach Pete seemed to gain a measure of life, of definition, like an empty glove abruptly filled by the flesh of a hand.

"If you will excuse me," he said, in Coach Pete's annoying tone of voice, walking past me, "I have a detention over which to preside."

"To preside over," I said, and snorted at his back. "Over which to preside. No one actually talks like that."

He turned his head and gave me a flat-eyed look. Then he rounded a corner and was gone.

I rubbed at the spot on my forehead between my eyebrows and tried to think.

I had a bad feeling that fighting this guy was going to be a losing proposition. In my experience, when someone gets their kids a supernatural supernanny, they don't pick pushovers. Among wizards, I'm pretty buff—but the world is full of bigger fish than me. More to the point, even if I fought the svartalf and won, it might drag the White Council of Wizards into a violent clash with Svartalfheim. I wouldn't want to have something like that on my conscience.

I wanted to protect the Pounder kid, and I wasn't going to back away from that. But how was I supposed to protect him from the Bully Brothers if they had a heavyweight on deck, ready to charge in swinging? That kind of brawl could spill over onto any nearby kids, and fast. I didn't want this to turn into a slugfest. That wouldn't help Irwin Pounder.

But what could I do? What options did I have? How could I act without dragging the svartalf into a confrontation?

I couldn't.

"Ah," I said to no one, lifting a finger in the air. "Aha!"

I grabbed my mop bucket and hurried toward the cafeteria.

The school emptied out fast, making the same transition every school does every day, changing from a place full of life and energy, of movement and noise, into a series of echoing chambers and empty halls. Teachers and staff seemed as eager to be gone as the students. Good. It was still possible that things would get ugly, and if they did, the fewer people around, the better.

By the time I went by the janitor's closet to pick up the few tools I'd brought with me and went to the cafeteria, my bucket's squeaking wheels were the loudest sound I could hear. I turned the corner at almost exactly the same time as the Bully Brothers appeared from the opposite end of the hall. They drew up short, and I could feel the weight of their eyes as they assessed me. I ignored them and went on inside.

Bigfoot Irwin was already inside the cafeteria, seated at a table, writing on a piece of paper. I recognized the kid's rigid, resigned posture, and it made my wrist ache just to see it: Coach Pete had him writing a sentence repetitively, probably something about being more careful with his lunch tray. The monster.

Coach Pete stood leaning against a wall, reading a sports magazine of some sort. Or at least, that was what he appeared to be doing. I had to wonder how much genuine interest a svartalf might have in the NBA. His eyes flicked up as I entered; I saw them go flat.

I set my mop and bucket aside and started sweeping the floors with a large dust broom. My janitorial form was perfect. I saw Coach Pete's jaw clench a couple of times, and then he walked over to me.

"What are you doing?" he asked.

"Sweeping the floor," I replied, guileless as a newborn.

"This is not a matter for levity," he said. "No amount of it will save your life."

"You grossly underestimate the power of laughter," I said. "But if there's some kind of violent altercation between students, any janitor in the world would find it his honor-bound duty to report it to the administration."

Coach Pete made a growling sound.

"Go ahead," I said. "Let your kids loose on him. I saw how they behaved in their classrooms. They're problem cases. Irwin's obviously a brilliant student and a good kid. When the administration finds out the three of them were involved in a fight, what do you think happens to the Troublemaker Twins? This is a private school. Out they go. Irwin is protected—and I won't have to lift a finger to interfere."

Coach Pete rolled up the magazine and tapped it against his leg a couple of times. Then he relaxed, and a small smile appeared upon his lips. "You are correct, of course, except for one thing."

"Yeah? What's that?"

"They will not be exiled. Their parents donate more funds to the school than any ten other families—and a great deal more than Irwin's mother could ever afford." He gave me a very small, very Gallic shrug. "This is a private school. The boys' parents paid for the cafeteria within which we stand."

I found myself gritting my teeth. "First of all, you have got to get over this fetish for grammatically correct prepositions. It makes you sound like a prissy twit. And second of all, money isn't everything."

"Money is power," he replied.

"Power isn't everything."

"No," he said, and his smile became smug. "It is the only thing."

I looked back out into the hallway through the open glass wall separating it from the cafeteria. The Bully Brothers were standing in the hall, staring at Irwin the way hungry lions stare at gazelles.

Coach Pete nodded pleasantly to me and returned to his original place by the wall, unrolling his magazine and opening it again.

"Dammit," I whispered. The svartalf might well be right. At an upper-class institution such as this, money and politics would have a ridiculous amount of influence. Whether aristocracies were hereditary or economic, they'd been successfully buying their children out of trouble for centuries. The Bully Brothers might well come out of this squeaky clean, and they'd be able to continue to persecute Bigfoot Irwin.

Maybe this would turn out to be a slugfest after all.

I swept my way over to Irwin's table and came to a stop. Then I sat down across from him.

He looked up from his page of scrawled sentences, and his face was pale. He wouldn't meet my eyes.

"How you doing, kid?" I asked him. When I spoke, he actually flinched a little.

"Fine," he mumbled.

Hell's bells. He was afraid of me. "Irwin," I said, keeping my voice gentle, "relax. I'm not going to hurt you."

"Okay," he said, without relaxing a bit.

"They've been doing this for a while now, haven't they?" I asked him.

"Um," he said.

"The Bully Brothers. The ones staring at you right now."

Irwin shivered and glanced aside without actually turning his head toward the window. "It's not a big deal."

"It kind of is," I said. "They've been giving you grief for a long time, haven't they? Only lately it's been getting worse. They've been scarier. More violent. Bothering you more and more often."

He said nothing, but something in his lack of reaction told me that I'd hit the nail on the head.

I sighed. "Irwin, my name is Harry Dresden. Your father sent me to help you."

That made his eyes snap up to me, and his mouth opened. "M-my...my dad?"

"Yeah," I said. "He can't be here to help you. So he asked me to do it for him."

"My dad," Irwin said, and I heard the ache in his voice, so poignant that my own chest tightened in empathy. I'd never known my mother, and my father died before I started going to school. I knew what it was like to have holes in my life in the shape of people who should have been there.

His eyes flicked toward the Bully Brothers again, though he didn't turn his head. "Sometimes," he said quietly, "if I ignore them, they go away." He stared down at his paper. "My dad...I mean, I never...you met him?"

"Yeah."

His voice was very small. "Is...is he nice?"

"Seems to be," I said gently.

"And...and he knows about me?"

"Yeah," I said. "He wants to be here for you. But he can't."

"Why not?" Irwin asked.

"It's complicated."

Irwin nodded and looked down. "Every Christmas there's a present from him. But I think maybe Mom is just writing his name on the tag."

"Maybe not," I said quietly. "He sent me. And I'm way more expensive than a present."

Irwin frowned at that and said, "What are you going to do?"

"That isn't the question you should be asking," I said.

"What is, then?"

I put my elbows on the table and leaned toward him. "The question, Irwin, is what are *you* going to do?"

"Get beat up, probably," he said.

"You can't keep hoping they'll just go away, kid," I said. "There are people out there who enjoy hurting and scaring others. They're going to keep doing it until you make them stop."

"I'm not going to fight anyone," Irwin all but whispered. "I'm not going to hurt anyone. I…I can't. And besides, if they're picking on me, they're not picking on anyone else."

I leaned back and took a deep breath, studying his hunched shoulders, his bowed head. The kid was frightened, the kind of fear that is planted and nurtured and which grows over the course of months and years. But there was also a kind of gentle, immovable resolve in the boy's skinny body. He wasn't afraid of facing the Bully Brothers. He just dreaded going through the pain that the encounter would bring.

Courage, like fear, comes in multiple varieties.

"Damn," I said quietly. "You got some heart, kiddo."

"Can you stay with me?" he asked. "If…if you're here, maybe they'll leave me alone."

"Today," I said quietly. "What about tomorrow?"

"I don't know," he said. "Are you going away?"

"Can't stay here forever," I replied. "Sooner or later you're going to be on your own."

"I won't fight," he said. A droplet of water fell from his bowed head to smear part of a sentence on his paper. "I won't be like them."

"Irwin," I said. "Look at me."

He lifted his eyes. They were full. He was blinking to keep more tears from falling.

"Fighting isn't always a bad thing."

"That's not what the school says."

I smiled briefly. "The school has liability to worry about. I only have to worry about you."

He frowned, his expression intent, pensive. "When isn't it a bad thing?"

"When you're protecting yourself, or someone else, from harm," I said. "When someone wants to hurt you or someone who can't defend themselves—and when the rightful authority can't or won't protect you."

"But you have to hurt people to win a fight. And that isn't right."

"No," I said. "It isn't. But sometimes it is necessary."

"It isn't necessary right now," he said. "I'll be fine. It'll hurt, but I'll be fine."

"Maybe you will," I said. "But what about when they're done with you? What happens when they decide that it was so much fun to hurt you, they go pick on someone else, too?"

"Do you think they'll do that?"

"Yes," I said. "That's how bullies work. They keep hurting people until someone makes them stop."

He fiddled with the pencil in his fingers. "I don't like fighting. I don't even like playing Street Fighter."

"This isn't really about fighting," I said. "It's about communication."

He frowned. "Huh?"

"They're doing something wrong," I said. "You need to communicate with them. Tell them that what they're doing isn't acceptable, and that they need to stop doing it."

"I've said that," he said. "I tried that a long time ago. It didn't work."

"You talked to them," I said. "It didn't get through. You need to find another way to get your message through. You have to show them."

"You mean hurt them."

"Not necessarily," I said quietly. "But guys like those two jokers only respect strength. If you show them that you have it, they'll get the idea."

Irwin frowned harder. "No one ever talked to me about it like that before."

"I guess not," I said.

"I'm...I'm scared of doing that."

"Who wouldn't be?" I asked him. "But the only way to beat your fears is to face them. If you don't, they're going to keep on doing this to you, and then others, and someday someone is going to get hurt bad. It might even be those two jackasses who get hurt—if someone doesn't make them realize that they can't go through life acting like that."

"They aren't really bad guys," Irwin said slowly. "I mean...to anyone but me. They're okay to other people."

"Then I'd say that you'd be helping them as well as yourself, Irwin."

He nodded slowly and took a deep breath. "I'll...I'll think about it."

"Good," I said. "Thinking for yourself is the most valuable skill you'll ever learn."

"Thank you, Harry," he said.

I rose and picked up my broom. "You bet."

I went back to sweeping one end of the cafeteria. Coach Pete stood at the other end. Irwin returned to his writing—and the Bully Brothers came in.

They approached as before, moving between the tables, splitting up to come at Irwin from two sides. They ignored me and Coach Pete, closing in on Irwin with impatient eagerness.

Irwin's pencil stopped scratching when they both were about five feet away from him, and without looking up he said in a sharp, firm voice, "Stop."

They did. I could see the face of only one of them, but the bully was blinking in surprise.

"This is not cool," Irwin said. "And I'm not going to let you do it anymore."

The brothers eyed him, traded rather feral smiles, and then each of them lunged at Irwin and grabbed an arm. They hauled him back with surprising speed and power, slamming his back onto the floor. One of them started slapping at his eyes and face while the other produced a short length of heavy rubber tubing, jerked Irwin's shirt up, and started hitting him on the stomach with the hose.

I gritted my teeth and reached for the handle of my mop— except it wasn't a mop that was poking up out of the bucket. It was my staff, a six-foot length of oak as thick as my circled thumb and forefinger. If this was how the Bully Brothers started the beating, I didn't even want to think about what they'd do for a finale. Svartalf or not, I couldn't allow things to go any further before I stepped in.

Coach Pete's dark eyes glittered at me from behind his sports magazine, and he crooked a couple of fingers on one hand in a way that no human being could have. I don't know what kind of magical energy the svartalf was using, but he was good with it. There was a sharp crackling sound, and the water in the mop bucket froze solid in an instant, trapping my staff in place.

My heart sped up. That kind of magical control was a bad, bad sign. It meant that the svartalf was better than me—probably a lot better. He hadn't used a focus of any kind to help him out, the way my staff would help me focus and control my own power. If we'd been fighting with swords, that move would have been the same as him clipping off the tips of my eyelashes without drawing blood. This guy would kill me if I fought him.

I set my jaw, grabbed the staff in both hands, and sent a surge of my will and power rushing down its rune-carved length into the entrapping ice. I muttered *"Forzare"* as I twisted the staff, and pure energy lashed out into the ice, pulverizing it into chunks the size of gravel.

Coach Pete leaned forward slightly, eager, and I saw his eyes gleam. Svartalves were old-school, and their culture had been born in the time of the Vikings. They thought mortal combat was at least as fun as it was scary, and their idea of mercy only embraced killing you quickly as opposed to killing you slowly. If I started up with this svartalf, it wouldn't be over until one of us was dead. Probably me. I was afraid.

The sound of the rubber hose hitting Irwin's stomach and the harsh breathing of the struggling children echoed in the large room.

I took a deep breath, grabbed my staff in two hands, and began drawing in my will once more.

And then Bigfoot Irwin roared, *"I said no!"*

The kid twisted his shoulders in an abrupt motion and tossed one of the brothers away as if he weighed no more than a soccer ball. The bully flew ten feet before his butt hit the ground. The second brother was still staring in shock when Bigfoot Irwin sat up, grabbed him by the front of his shirt, and rose. He lifted the second brother's feet off the floor and simply held him there, scowling furiously up at him.

The Bully Brothers had inherited their predatory instinct from their supernatural parent.

Bigfoot Irwin had gotten something else.

The second brother stared down at the younger boy and struggled to wriggle free, his face pale and frantic. Irwin didn't let him go.

"Hey, look at me," Irwin snarled. "This is not okay. You were mean to me. You kept hurting me. For no reason. That's over. Now. I'm not going to let you do it anymore. Okay?"

The first brother sat up shakily from the floor and stared agog at his former victim, now holding his brother effortlessly off the floor.

"Did you hear me?" Irwin asked, giving the kid a little shake. I heard his teeth clack together.

"Y-yeah," stammered the dangling brother, nodding emphatically. "I hear you. I hear you. We hear you."

Irwin scowled for a moment. Then he gave the second brother a push before releasing him. The bully fell to the floor three feet away and scrambled quickly back from Irwin. The pair of them started a slow retreat.

"I mean it," Irwin said. "What you've been doing isn't cool. We'll figure out something else for you to do for fun. Okay?"

The Bully Brothers mumbled something vaguely affirmative and then hurried out of the cafeteria.

Bigfoot Irwin watched them go. Then he looked down at his hands, turning them over and back as if he'd never seen them before.

I kept my grip on my staff and looked down the length of the cafeteria at Coach Pete. I arched an eyebrow at him. "It seems like the boys sorted this out on their own."

Coach Pete lowered his magazine slowly. The air was thick with tension, and the silence was its hard surface.

Then the svartalf said, "Your sentences, Mr. Pounder."

"Yessir, Coach Pete," Irwin said. He turned back to the table and sat down, and his pencil started scratching at the paper again.

Coach Pete nodded at him, then came over to me. He stood facing me for a moment, his expression blank.

"I didn't intervene," I said. "I didn't try to dissuade your boys from following their natures. Irwin did that."

The svartalf pursed his lips thoughtfully and then nodded slowly. "Technically accurate. And yet you still had a hand in what just happened. Why should I not exact retribution for your interference?"

"Because I just helped your boys."

"In what way?"

"Irwin and I taught them caution—that some prey is too much for them to handle. And we didn't even hurt them to make it happen."

Coach Pete considered that for a moment and then gave me a faint smile. "A lesson best learned early rather than late." He turned and started to walk away.

"Hey," I said in a sharp, firm voice.

He paused.

"You took the kid's book today," I said. "Please return it."

Irwin's pencil scratched along the page, suddenly loud.

Coach Pete turned. Then he pulled the paperback in question out of his pocket and flicked it through the air. I caught it in one hand, which probably made me look a lot more cool and collected than I felt at the time.

Coach Pete inclined his head to me, a little more deeply than before. "Wizard."

I mirrored the gesture. "Svartalf."

He left the cafeteria, shaking his head. What sounded suspiciously like a chuckle bubbled in his wake.

I waited until Irwin was done with his sentences, and then I walked him to the front of the building, where his maternal grandmother was waiting to pick him up.

"Was that okay?" he asked me. "I mean, did I do right?"

"Asking me if I thought you did right isn't the question," I said.

Irwin suddenly smiled at me. "Do I think I did right?" He nodded slowly. "I think...I think I do."

"How's it feel?" I asked him.

"It feels good. I feel...not happy. Satisfied. Whole."

"That's how it's supposed to feel," I said. "Whenever you've got a choice, do good, kiddo. It isn't always fun or easy, but in the long run it makes your life better."

He nodded, frowning thoughtfully. "I'll remember."

"Cool," I said.

He offered me his hand very seriously, and I shook it. He had a strong grip for a kid. "Thank you, Harry. Could...could I ask you a favor?"

"Sure."

"If you see my dad again...could you tell him...could you tell him I did good?"

"Of course," I said. "I think what you did will make him very proud."

That all but made the kid glow. "And...and tell him that... that I'd like to meet him. You know. Someday."

"Will do," I said quietly.

Bigfoot Irwin nodded at me. Then he turned and made his gangly way over to the waiting car and slid into it. I stood and watched until the car was out of sight. Then I rolled my bucket of ice back into the school so that I could go home.

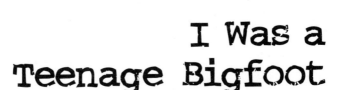

I Was a
Teenage Bigfoot

Takes place circa *Dead Beat*

There are times when, as a professional wizard, my vocation calls me to the great outdoors, and that night I was in the northwoods of Wisconsin with a mixed pack of researchers, enthusiasts and...well. Nerds.

"I don't know, man," said a skinny kid named Nash. "What's his name again?"

I poked the small campfire I'd set up earlier with a stick and pretended that they weren't standing less than ten feet away from me. The forest made forest sounds like it was supposed to. Full dark had fallen less than half an hour before.

"Harry Dresden," said Gary, a plump kid with a cell phone, a GPS unit, and some kind of video game device on his belt. "Supposed to be a psychic or something." He was twiddling deft fingers over the surface of what they call a "smart" phone, these days. Hell, the damned things are probably smarter than me.

"Supposed to have helped Chicago PD a bunch of times. I'd pull up the Internet references, but I can't get reception out here."

"A psychic?" Nash said. "How is anyone ever supposed to take our research seriously if we keep showing up with fruit-cakes like that?"

Gary shrugged. "Doctor Sinor knows him or something."

Doctor Sinor had nearly been devoured by an ogre in a suburban park one fine summer evening, and I'd gotten her out in one piece. Like most people who have a brush with the supernatural, she'd rationalized the truth away as rapidly as possible—which had led her to participate in such fine activities as tonight's Bigfoot expedition in her spare time.

"Gentlemen," Sinor said, impatiently. She was a blocky, no-nonsense type, grey-haired and straight-backed. "If you could help me with these speakers, we might actually manage to blast a call or two before dawn."

Gary and Nash both hustled over to the edge of the firelight to start messing about with the equipment the troop of researchers had packed in. There were half a dozen of them, altogether, all of them busy with trail cameras and call blasting speakers and scent markers and audio recorders.

I pulled a sandwich out of my pocket and started eating it. I took my time about it. I was in no hurry.

For those of you who don't know it, a forest at night is *dark*. Sometimes pitch-black. There was no moon to speak of in the sky, and the light of the stars doesn't make it more than a few inches into a mixed canopy of deciduous trees and evergreens. The light from my little campfire and the hand-held flashlights of the researchers soon gave the woods all the light there was.

Their equipment wasn't working very well—my bad, probably. Modern technology doesn't get on well with the magically gifted. For about an hour, nothing much happened beyond the slapping of mosquitoes and a lot of electronic noises squawking from the loudspeakers.

Then the researchers got everything online and went through their routine. They played primate calls over the speakers and then dutifully recorded the forest afterward. Everything broke down again. The researchers soldiered on, repairing things, and eventually Gary tried wood-knocking, which meant banging on trees with fallen limbs and waiting to hear if there was a response.

I liked Doctor Sinor, but I had asked to come strictly as a ride-along and I didn't pitch in with her team's efforts.

The whole "let's find Bigfoot" thing seems a little ill-planned to me, personally. Granted, my perspective is different from that of non-wizards, but marching out into the woods looking for a very large and very powerful creature by blasting out what you're pretty sure are territorial challenges to fight (or else mating calls) seems...somewhat unwise.

I mean, if there's no Bigfoot, no problem. But what if you're standing there, screaming "Bring it on!" and *find* a Bigfoot?

Worse yet, what if *he* finds *you*?

Even worse, what if you were screaming, "Do me, baby!" and he finds you *then*?

Is it me? Am I crazy? Or does the whole thing just seem like a recipe for trouble?

So anyway, while I kept my little fire going, the Questionably Wise Research Variety Act continued until after midnight. That's when I looked up to see a massive form standing at the edge of the trees, in the very outskirts of the light of my dying fire.

I'm in the ninety-ninth percentile for height, myself, but this guy was *tall*. My head might have come up to his collarbone, barely, assuming I had correctly estimated where his collarbone was under the long, shaggy, dark brown hair covering him. It wasn't long enough to hide the massive weight of muscle he carried on that enormous frame or the simple, disturbing, very slightly inhuman proportions of his body. His face was broad, blunt, with a heavy brow ridge that turned his eyes into mere gleams of reflected light.

Most of all, there was a sense of awesome power granted to his presence by his size alone, chilling even to someone who had seen big things in action before. There's a reaction to something that much bigger than you, an automatic assumption of menace that is built into the human brain: Big equals dangerous.

It took about fifteen seconds before the first researcher, Gary I think, noticed and let out a short gasp. In my peripheral vision, I saw the entire group turn toward the massive form by the fire and freeze into place. The silence was brittle crystal.

I broke it by bolting up from my seat and letting out a high-pitched shriek.

Half a dozen other screams joined it, and I whirled as if to flee, only to see Doctor Sinor and crew hotfooting it down the path we'd followed into the woods, back toward the cars.

I held it in for as long as I could, and only after I was sure that they wouldn't hear it did I let loose the laughter bubbling in my chest. I sank back onto my log by the fire, laughing, and beckoning the large form forward.

"Harry," rumbled the figure in a very, very deep voice, the words marked with the almost indefinable clippings of a Native American accent. "You have an unsophisticated sense of humor."

"I can't help it," I said, wiping at tears of laughter. "It never gets old." I waved to the open ground across the fire from me. "Sit, sit, be welcome, big brother."

"Appreciate it," rumbled the giant and squatted down across the fire from me, touching fingers the size of cucumbers to his heart in greeting. His broad, blunt face was amused. "So. Got any smokes?"

It wasn't the first time I'd done business with the Forest People. They're old school. There's a certain way one goes about business with someone considered a peer, and Strength of a River in His Shoulders was an old school kind of guy. There were proprieties to be observed.

So we shared a thirty-dollar cigar, which I'd brought, had some S'mores, which I made, and sipped from identical plastic bottles of Coca-Cola, which I had purchased. By the time we were done, the fire had burned down to glowing embers, which suited me fine—and I knew that River Shoulders would be more comfortable in the near-dark, too. I didn't mind being the one to provide everything. It would have been a hassle for River Shoulders to do it, and we'd probably be smoking, eating, and drinking raw and unpleasant things if he had.

Besides, it was worth it. The Forest People had been around long before the great gold rushes of the nineteenth century, and they were loaded. River Shoulders had paid my retainer with a gold nugget the size of a golf ball, the last time I'd done business with him.

"Your friends," he said, nodding toward the disappeared researchers. "They going to come back?"

"Not before dawn," I said. "For all they know, you *got* me."

River Shoulders' chest rumbled with a sound that was both amused and not entirely pleased. "Like my people don't have enough stigmas already."

"You want to clear things up, I can get you on the Larry Fowler show any time you want."

River Shoulders shuddered—given his size, it was a lot of shuddering. "TV rots the brains of people who see it. Don't even want to know what it does to the people who *make* it."

I snorted. "I got your message," I said. "I am here."

"And so you are," he said. He frowned, an expression that was really sort of terrifying on his features. I didn't say anything. You just don't rush the Forest People. They're patient on an almost alien level, compared to human beings, and I knew that our meeting was already being conducted with unseemly haste, by River Shoulders' standards. Finally, he swigged a bit more Coke, the bottle looking tiny in his vast hands, and sighed. "There is a problem with my son. Again."

I sipped some Coke and nodded, letting a little time pass before I answered. "Irwin was a fine, strong boy when I last saw him."

The conversation continued with contemplative pauses between each bit of speech. "He is sick."

"Children sometimes grow sick."

"Not children of the Forest People."

"What, never?"

"No, never. And I will not quote Gilbert and Sullivan."

"Their music was silly and fine."

River Shoulders nodded agreement. "Indeed."

"What can you tell me of your son's sickness?"

"His mother tells me the school's doctor says he has something called mah-no."

"Mono," I said. "It is a common illness. It is not dangerous."

"An illness could not touch one born of the Forest People," River Shoulders rumbled.

"Not even one with only one parent of your folk?" I asked.

"Indeed," he said. "Something else must therefore be happening. I am concerned for Irwin's safety."

The fire let out a last crackle and a brief, gentle flare of light, showing me River Shoulders clearly. His rough features were touched with the same quiet worry I'd seen on dozens and dozens of my clients' faces.

"He still doesn't know who you are, does he."

The giant shifted his weight slightly as if uncomfortable. "Your society is, to me, irrational and bewildering. Which is good. Can't have everyone the same, or the earth would get boring."

I thought about it for a moment and then said, "You feel he has problems enough to deal with already."

River Shoulders spread his hands, as if my own words had spotlighted the truth.

I nodded, thought about it, and said, "We aren't that different. Even among my people, a boy misses his father."

"A voice on a telephone is not a father," he said.

"But it is more than nothing," I said. "I have lived with a father and without a father. With one was better."

The silence stretched extra-long.

"In time," the giant responded, very quietly. "For now, my concern is his physical safety. I cannot go to him. I spoke to his mother. We ask someone we trust to help us learn what is happening."

I didn't agree with River Shoulders about talking to his kid, but that didn't matter. He wasn't hiring me to get parenting advice, about which I had no experience to call upon anyway. He needed help looking out for the kid. So I'd do what I could to help him. "Where can I find Irwin?"

"Chicago," he said. "St. Mark's Academy for the Gifted and Talented."

"Boarding school. I know the place." I finished the Coke and rose. "It will be my pleasure to help the Forest People once again."

The giant echoed my actions, standing. "Already had your retainer sent to your account. By morning, his mother will have granted you the power of a turnkey."

It took me a second to translate River Shoulders' imperfect understanding of mortal society. "Power of attorney," I corrected him.

"That," he agreed.

"Give her my best."

"Will," he said, and touched his thick fingertips to his massive chest.

I put my fingertips to my heart in reply and nodded up to my client. "I'll start in the morning."

It took me most of the rest of the night to get back down to Chicago, go to my apartment, and put on my suit. I'm not a suit guy. For one thing, when you're NBA sized, you don't exactly get to buy them off the rack. For another, I just don't like them—but sometimes they're a really handy disguise, when I want people to mistake me for someone grave and responsible. So I put on the grey suit with a crisp white shirt and a clip-on tie, and headed down to St. Mark's.

The academy was an upper-end place in the suburbs north of Chicago, and was filled with the offspring of the city's luminaries. They had their own small, private security force. They had wrought iron gates and brick walls and ancient trees and ivy. They had multiple buildings on the grounds, like a miniature university campus, and, inevitably, they had an administration building. I started there.

It took me a polite quarter of an hour to get the lady in the front office to pick up the fax granting me power of attorney from Irwin's mom, the archeologist, who was in the field somewhere in Canada. It included a description of me, and I produced both my ID and my investigator's license. It took me another half an hour of waiting to be admitted to the office of the dean, Doctor Fabio.

"Doctor Fabio," I said. I fought valiantly not to titter when I did.

Fabio did not offer me a seat. He was a good-looking man of sober middle age, and his eyes told me that he did not approve of me in the least, even though I was wearing the suit.

"Ms. Pounder's son is in our infirmary, receiving care from a highly experienced nurse practitioner and a physician who visits three days a week," Doctor Fabio told me, when I had explained my purpose. "I assure you he is well cared for."

"I'm not the one who needs to be assured of anything," I replied. "His mother is."

"Then your job here is finished," said Fabio.

I shook my head. "I kinda need to see him, Doctor."

"I see no need to disrupt either Irwin's recovery or our academic routine, Mister Dresden," Fabio replied. "Our students receive some of the most intensive instruction in the world. It demands a great deal of focus and drive."

"Kids are resilient," I said. "And I'll be quiet like a mouse. They'll never know I was there."

"I'm sorry," he replied, "but I am not amenable to random investigators wandering the grounds."

I nodded seriously. "Okay. In that case, I'll report to Doctor Pounder that you refused to allow her duly appointed representative to see her son, and that I cannot confirm his well-being. At which point I am confident that she will either radio for a plane to pick her up from her dig site, or else backpack her way out. I think the good doctor will view this with alarm and engage considerable maternal protective instinct." I squinted at Fabio. "Have you actually *met* Doctor Pounder?"

He scowled at me.

"She's about yay tall," I said, putting a hand at the level of my temples. "And she works outdoors for a living. She looks like she could wrestle a Sasquatch." Heh. Among other things.

"Are you threatening me?" Doctor Fabio asked.

I smiled. "I'm telling you that I'm way less of a disruption than Mama Bear will be. She'll be a headache for weeks. Give me half an hour, and then I'm gone."

Fabio glowered at me.

St. Mark's infirmary was a spotless, well-ordered place, located immediately adjacent to its athletics building. I was walked there by a young man named Steve, who wore a spotless, well-ordered security uniform.

Steve rapped his knuckles on the frame of the open doorway and said, "Visitor to see Mister Pounder."

A young woman who looked entirely too nice for the likes of Doctor Fabio and Steve looked up from a crossword puzzle. She had chestnut-colored hair, rimless glasses, and had a body that could be readily appreciated even beneath her cheerfully patterned scrubs.

"Well," I said. "Hello, nurse."

"I can't think of a sexier first impression than a man quoting Yakko and Wakko Warner," she said, her tone dry.

I sauntered in and offered her my hand. "Me neither. Harry Dresden, PI."

"Jen Gerard. There are some letters that go after, but I used them all on the crossword." She shook my hand and eyed Steve. "Everyone calls me Nurse Jen. The flying monkeys let you in, eh?"

Steve looked professionally neutral. He folded his arms.

Nurse Jen flipped her wrists at him. "Shoo, shoo. If I'm suddenly attacked I'll scream like a girl."

"No visitors without a security presence," Steve said firmly.

"Unless they're richer than a guy in a cheap suit," Nurse Jen said archly. She smiled sweetly at Steve and shut the infirmary door. It all but bumped the end of his nose. She turned back to me and said, "Doctor Pounder sent you?"

"She's at a remote location," I said. "She wanted someone to get eyes on her son and make sure he was okay. And for the record, it wasn't cheap."

Nurse Jen snorted and said, "Yeah, I guess a guy your height doesn't get to shop off the rack, does he." She led me across the first room of the infirmary, which had a first aid station and an examination table, neither of which looked as though they got a lot of use. There were a couple of rooms attached. One was a bathroom. The other held what looked like the full gear of a hospital's intensive care ward, including an automated bed.

Bigfoot Irwin lay asleep on the bed. It had been a few years since I'd seen him, but I recognized him. He was fourteen years old and over six feet tall, filling the length of the bed, and he had the scrawny look of young things that aren't done growing.

Nurse Jen went to his side and shook his shoulder gently. The kid blinked his eyes open and muttered something. Then he looked at me.

"Harry," he said. "What are you doing here?"

"Sup, kid," I said. "I heard you were sick. Your mom asked me to stop by."

He smiled faintly. "Yeah. This is what I get for staying in Chicago instead of going up to British Columbia with her."

"And think of all the Spam you missed eating."

Irwin snorted, closed his eyes, and said, "Tell her I'm fine. Just need to rest." Then he apparently started doing exactly that.

Nurse Jen eased silently out of the room and herded me gently away. Then she spread her hands. "He's been like that. Sleeping maybe twenty hours a day."

"Is that normal for mono?" I asked.

I WAS A TEENAGE BIGFOOT

"Not so much," Nurse Jen said. She shook her head. "Though it's not completely unheard of. That's just a preliminary diagnosis based on his symptoms. He needs some lab work to be sure."

"Fabio isn't allowing it," I said.

She waggled a hand. "He isn't paying for it. The state of the economy, the school's earnings last quarter, et cetera. And the doctor was sure it was mono."

"You didn't tell his mom about that?" I asked.

"I never spoke to her. Doctor Fabio handles all of the communication with the parents. Gives it that personal touch. Besides. I'm just the nurse practitioner. The official physician said mono, so behold, it is mono."

I grunted. "Is the boy in danger?"

She shook her head. "If I thought that, to hell with Fabio and the winged monkeys. I'd drive the kid to a hospital myself. But just because he isn't in danger now doesn't mean he won't be if nothing is done. It's probably mono. But."

"But you don't take chances with a kid's health," I said.

She folded her arms. "Exactly. Especially when his mother is so far away. There's an issue of trust, here."

I nodded. Then I said, "How invasive are the tests?"

"Blood samples. Fairly straightforward."

I chewed that one over for a moment. Irwin's blood was unlikely to be exactly the same as human blood, though who knew how intensively they would have to test it to realize that. Scions of mortal and supernatural pairings had created no enormous splash in the scientific community, and they'd been around for as long as humanity itself, which suggested that any differences weren't easy to spot. It seemed like a reasonable risk to take, all things considered, especially if River Shoulders was maybe wrong about Irwin's immunity to disease.

And besides. I needed some time alone to work.

"Do the tests, on my authority. Assuming the kid is willing, I mean."

Nurse Jen frowned as I began to speak, then nodded at the second sentence. "Okay."

Nurse Jen woke up Irwin long enough to explain the tests, make sure he was okay with them, and take a couple of little vials of blood from his arm. She left to take the vials to a nearby lab and left me sitting with Irwin.

"How's life, kid?" I asked him. "Any more bully problems?"

Irwin snorted weakly. "No, not really. Though, they don't use their fists for that, here. And there's a lot more of them."

"That's what they call civilization," I said. "It's still better than the other way."

"One thing's the same. You show them you aren't afraid, they leave you alone."

"They do," I said. "Coward's a coward, whether he's throwing punches or words."

Irwin smiled and closed his eyes again.

I gave the kid a few minutes to be sound asleep before I got to work.

River Shoulders hadn't asked for my help because I was the only decent person in Chicago. The last time Irwin had problems, they'd had their roots in the supernatural side of reality. Clearly, the giant thought that this problem was similar, and he was smarter than the vast majority of human beings, including me. I'd be a fool to discount his concerns. I didn't think there was anything more troublesome than a childhood illness at hand, but I was going to cover my bases. That's what being professional means.

I'd brought what I needed in the pockets of my suit. I took out a small baggie of powdered quartz crystal and a piece of paper inscribed with runes written in ink infused with the same powder and folded into a fan. I stood over Irwin and took a moment to focus my thoughts, both upon the spell I was about to work and upon the physical coordination it would require.

I took a deep breath, then flicked the packet of quartz dust into the air at the same time I swept the rune-inscribed fan through a strong arc, released my will, and murmured, "*Optio.*"

Light kindled in the spreading cloud of fine dust, a flickering glow that spread with the cloud, sparkling through the full spectrum of visible colors in steady, pulsing waves. It was beautiful magic, which was rare for me. I mean, explosions and lightning bolts and so on were pretty standard fare. This kind of gentle, interrogative spell? It was a treat to have a reason to use it.

As the cloud of dust settled gently over the sleeping boy, the colors began to swirl as the spell interacted with his aura, the energy of life that surrounds all living things. Irwin's aura was bloody strong, standing out several inches farther from his body than on most humans. I was a full-blown wizard, and a strong one, and my aura wasn't any more powerful. That would be his father's blood, then. The Forest People were in possession of potent magic, which was one reason no one ever seemed to get a decent look at one of them. Irwin had begun to develop a reservoir of energy to rival that of anyone on the White Council of wizardry.

That was likely the explanation for Irwin's supposed immunity to disease—the aura of life around him was simply too strong to be overwhelmed by a mundane germ or virus. Supported by that kind of energy, his body's immune system would simply whale on any invaders. It probably also explained Irwin's size, his growing body drawing upon the raw power of his aura to optimize whatever growth potential was in his mixed genes. Thinking about it, it might even explain the length of River Shoulders' body hair, which just goes to show that no supernatural ability is perfect.

Oh, and as the dust settled against Irwin's body, it revealed threads of black sorcery laced throughout his aura, pulsing and throbbing with a disturbing, seething energy.

I nearly fell out of my chair in sheer surprise.

"Oh no," I muttered. "The kid couldn't just have gotten mono. That would be way too easy."

I called up a short, gentle wind to scatter the quartz dust from Bigfoot Irwin's covers and pajamas, and then sat back for a moment to think.

The kid had been hit with black magic. Not only that, but it had been done often enough that it had left track marks in his aura. Some of those threads of dark sorcery were fresh ones, probably inflicted at some point during the previous night.

Most actions of magic aren't any more terribly mysterious or complicated than physical actions. In fact, a lot of what happens in magic can be described by basic concepts of physics. Energy can neither be created nor destroyed, for example—but it *can* be moved. The seething aura of life around the young scion represented a significant force of energy.

A *very* significant source.

Someone had been siphoning energy off of Bigfoot Irwin. The incredible vital aura around the kid now was, I realized, only a fraction of what it *should* have been. Someone had been draining the kid of that energy and using it for something else. A vampire of some kind? Maybe. The White Court of Vampires drained the life-energy from their victims, though they mostly did it through physical contact, mostly sexual congress, and there would be really limited opportunity for that sort of thing in a strictly monitored coed boarding school. Irwin had been attacked both frequently and regularly, to have his aura be so mangled.

I could sweep the place for a vampire. Maybe. They were not easy to spot. I couldn't discount a vamp completely, because they were definitely one of the usual suspects, but had it been one of the White Court after the kid, his aura would have been more damaged in certain areas than others. Instead, his aura had been equally diminished all around. That would indicate, if not conclusively prove, some kind of attack that was entirely nonphysical.

I settled back in my chair to wait, watching Bigfoot Irwin sleep. I'd stay alert for any further attack, at least until Nurse Jen got back.

River Shoulders was right. This wasn't illness. Someone was killing the kid very, very slowly.

I wasn't going to leave him alone.

Nurse Jen came back in a little less than two hours. She looked at me with her eyebrows raised and said, "You're still here."

"Looks like," I said. "What was I supposed to do?"

"Leave me a number to call with the results," she said.

I winked at her. "If it makes you feel any better, I can still do that."

"I'm taking a break from dating cartoon characters and the children who love them." She held up the envelope and said, "It's mono."

I blinked. "It is?"

She nodded and sighed. "Definitely. An acute case, apparently, but it's mono."

I nodded slowly, thinking. It might make sense, if Irwin's immune system had come to rely upon the energy of his aura. The attacks had diminished his aura, which had in turn diminished his body's capacity to resist disease. Instead of fighting off an illness when exposed, his weakened condition had resulted in an infection—and it was entirely possible that his body had never had any practice in fighting off something that had taken hold.

Nurse Jen tilted her head to one side and said, "What are you thinking?"

"How bad is it?" I asked her. "Does he need to go to a hospital?"

"He's in one," she said. "Small, but we have everything here that you'd find at a hospital, short of a ventilator. As long as his condition doesn't get any worse, he'll be fine."

Except that he wouldn't be fine. If the drain on his life-energy kept up, he might never have the strength he'd need to fight off this disease—and every other germ that happened to wander by.

I was thinking that the boy was defenseless—and I was the only one standing between Bigfoot Irwin and whatever was killing him.

I looked at Nurse Jen and said, "I need to use a phone."

"How serious?" Doctor Pounder asked. Her voice was scratchy. She was speaking to me over a HAM radio from somewhere in the wilds of unsettled Canada, and was shouting to make herself heard over the static and the patch between the radio and the phone.

"Potentially very serious," I half-shouted back. "I think you need to come here immediately!"

"He's that ill?" she asked.

"Yeah, Doc," I replied. "There could be complications, and I don't think he should be alone."

"I'm on the way. There's weather coming in. It might be tomorrow or the next day."

"Understood," I said. "I'll stay with him until then."

"You're a good man, Dresden," she said. "Thank you. I'll move as fast as I can. Pounder, out."

I hung up the phone and Nurse Jen stared at me with her mouth open. "What the hell are you doing?"

"My job," I replied calmly.

"The boy is going to be fine," Jen said. "He's not feeling great, but he'll be better soon enough. I told you, it's mono."

"There's more going on than that," I said.

"Oh?" Jen asked. "Like what?"

Explaining would just convince her I was a lunatic. "I'm not entirely at liberty to say. Doctor Pounder can explain when she arrives."

"If there's a health concern, I need to know about it now." She folded her arms. "Otherwise, maybe I should let the winged monkeys know that you're a problem."

"I told his mother I would stay with him."

"You told his mother a lot of things."

"What happened to not taking chances?"

"I'm thinking I'll start with you."

I felt tired. I needed sleep. I inhaled and exhaled slowly.

"Nurse," I said. "I care about the kid, too. I don't dispute your medical knowledge or authority over him. I just want to stay close to him until his mom gets here. That's why I was hired."

Nurse Jen eyed me askance. "What do you mean, it's more than mono?"

I folded my arms. "Um. Irwin is a nice guy. Would you agree with that?"

"Sure, he's a great kid. A real sweetheart, thoughtful."

I nodded. "And he has a tendency to attract the attention of... how do I put this?"

"Complete assholes?" Nurse Jen suggested.

"Exactly," I said. "People who mistake kindness for weakness."

She frowned. "Are you suggesting that his sickness is the result of a deliberate action?"

"I'm saying that I don't know that it isn't," I said. "And until I know, one way or another, I'm sticking close to the kid until the Doc gets here."

She continued looking skeptical. "You won't if I don't think you should. I don't care how much paperwork you have supporting you. If I start yelling, the winged monkeys will carry you right out to the street."

"They'd try," I said calmly.

She blinked at me. "You're a big guy. But you aren't that big."

"You might be surprised," I said. I leaned forward and said, very quietly, "I'm not. Leaving. The kid."

Nurse Jen's expression changed slowly, from skepticism to something very thoughtful. "You mean that, don't you."

"Every word."

She nodded. Then she called, "Steve."

The security guard lumbered into the room from the hall outside.

"Mister Dresden will be staying with Mister Pounder for a little while. Could you please ask the cafeteria to send over two dinner plates instead of one?"

Steve frowned, maybe trying to remember how to count all the way to two. Then he glowered at me, muttered a surly affirmative, and left, speaking quietly into his radio as he went.

"Thank you," I said. "For the food."

"You're lying to me," she said levelly. "Aren't you."

"I'm not telling you the whole truth," I said. "Subtle difference."

"Semantic difference," she said.

"But you're letting me stay anyway," I noted. "Why?"

She studied my face for a moment. Then she said, "I believe that you want to take care of Irwin."

The food was very good—nothing like the school cafeterias I remembered. Of course, I went to public school. Irwin woke up long enough to devour a trayful of food, and some of mine. He went to the bathroom, walking unsteadily, and then dropped back into an exhausted slumber. Nurse Jen stayed near, checking him frequently, taking his temperature in his ear every hour so that she didn't need to waken him.

I wanted to sleep, but I didn't need it yet. I might not have had the greatest academic experience, in childhood, but the other things I'd been required to learn had made me more ready for the eat-or-be-eaten portions of life than just about anyone. My record for going without sleep was just under six days, but I was pretty sure I could go longer if I had to. I could have napped in my chair, but I didn't want to take the chance that some kind of attack might happen while I was being lazy.

So I sat by Bigfoot Irwin and watched the shadows lengthen and swell into night.

The attack came just after nine o'clock.

Nurse Jen was taking Irwin's temperature again when I felt the sudden surge of cold, somehow oily energy flood the room.

Irwin took a sudden, shallow breath, and his face became very pale. Nurse Jen frowned at the digital thermometer she had in his ear. It suddenly emitted a series of beeping, wailing noises, and she jerked it free of Irwin just as a bunch of sparks drizzled from its battery casing. She dropped it to the floor, where it lay trailing a thin wisp of smoke.

"What the hell?" Nurse Jen demanded.

I rose to my feet, looking around the room. "Use a mercury thermometer next time," I said. I didn't have much in the way of magical gear on me, but I wasn't going to need any for this. I could feel the presence of the dark, dangerous magic, radiating through the room like the heat from a nearby fire.

Nurse Jen had pressed a stethoscope against Irwin's chest, listening for a moment, while I went to the opposite side of the bed and waved my hand through the air over the bed with my eyes closed, trying to orient upon the spell attacking Irwin's aura, so that I could backtrack it to its source.

"What are you doing?" Nurse Jen demanded.

"Inexplicable stuff," I said. "How is he?"

"Something isn't right," she said. "I don't think he's getting enough air. It's like an asthma attack." She put the stethoscope down and turned to a nearby closet, ripping out a small oxygen tank. She immediately began hooking up a line to it, attached to one of those nose-and-mouth-covering things, opened the valve, and pressed the cup down over Irwin's nose and mouth.

"Excuse me," I said, squeezing past her in order to wave my hand through the air over that side of the bed. I got a fix on the direction of the spell, and jabbed my forefinger in that direction. "What's that way?"

She blinked and stared at me incredulously. "What?"

"That way," I said, thrusting my finger in the indicated direction several times. "What is over that way?"

She frowned, shook her head a little, and said, "Uh, uh, the cafeteria and administration."

"Administration, eh?" I said. "Not the dorms?"

"No. They're the opposite way."

"You got any lunch ladies that hate Irwin?"

Nurse Jen looked at me like I was a lunatic. "What the hell are you talking about? No, of course not!"

I grunted. This attack clearly wasn't the work of a vampire, and the destruction of the electronic thermometer indicated the presence of mortal magic. The kids were required to be back in their dorms at this time, so it presumably wasn't one of them. And if it wasn't someone in the cafeteria, then it had to be someone in the administration building.

Doctor Fabio had been way too interested in making sure I wasn't around. If it was Fabio behind the attacks on Irwin, then I could probably expect some interference to be arriving—

The door to the infirmary opened, and Steve and two of his fellow security guards clomped into the room.

—any time now.

"You," Steve said, pointing a thick finger at me. "It's after free hours. No visitors on the grounds after nine. You're gonna have to go."

I eased back around Nurse Jen and out of the room Irwin was in. "Um," I said, "let me think about that."

Steve scowled. He had a very thick neck. So did his two buddies. "Second warning, sir. You are now trespassing on private property. If you do not leave immediately, the police will be summoned and you will be detained until their arrival."

"Shouldn't you be out making sure the boys aren't sneaking over to the girls' dorms and vice versa? Cause I'm thinking that's really more your speed, Steve."

Steve's face got red. "That's it," he said. "You are being detained until the police arrive, smartass."

"Let's don't do this," I said. "Seriously. You guys don't want to ride this train."

In answer, Steve snapped his hand out to one side, and one of those collapsible fighting batons extended to its full length and locked. His two friends followed suit.

"Wow," I said. "Straight to the weapons? Really? Completely inappropriate escalation." I held up my right hand, palm out. "I'm telling you, fellas. Don't try it."

Steve took two quick steps toward me, raising the baton.

I unleashed the will I had been gathering and murmured, "*Forzare.*"

Invisible force lashed out and slammed into Steve like a runaway car made of foam rubber. It lifted him off his feet and tossed him back, between his two buddies, and out the door of the infirmary. He hit the floor and lost a lot of his velocity before fetching up against the opposite wall with an explosion of expelled breath.

"Wah," I said, Bruce Lee style, and looked at the other two goons. "You boys want a choo-choo ride, too?"

The pair of them looked at me and then at each other, gripping their batons until their knuckles turned white. They hadn't had a clear view of exactly what had happened to Steve, since his body would have blocked them from it. For all they knew, I'd used some kind of judo on him. The pair of them came to a conclusion somewhere in there—that whatever I had pulled on Steve wouldn't work on both of them—and they began to rush me.

They thought wrong. I repeated the spell, only with twice the energy.

One of them went out the door, crashing into Steve, who had just been about to regain his feet. My control wasn't so good without any of my magical implements, though. The second man hit the side of the doorway squarely, and his head made the metal frame ring as it bounced off. The man's legs went rubbery and he staggered, bleeding copiously from a wound that was up above his hairline.

The second spell was more than the lights could handle, and the fluorescents in the infirmary exploded in showers of sparks and went out. Red-tinged emergency lights clicked on a few seconds later.

I checked around me. Nurse Jen was staring at me with her eyes wide. The wounded guard was on his back, rocking back and forth in obvious pain. The two who had been knocked into the hallway were still on the ground, staring at me in much the same way as Jen, except that Steve was clearly trying to get his radio to work. It wouldn't. It had folded when the lights did.

I spread my hands and said, to Nurse Jen, "I told them, didn't I? You heard me. Better take care of that guy."

Then I scowled, shook my head, and stalked off along the spell's back-trail, toward the administration building.

The doors to the building were locked, which was more the academy's problem than mine. I exercised restraint. I didn't take the doors off their hinges. I only ripped them off of their locks.

The door to Doctor Fabio's office was locked, and though I tried to exercise restraint, I've always had issues with controlling my power—especially when I'm angry. This time, I tore the door off its hinges, slamming it down flat to the floor inside the office as if smashed in by a medieval battering ram.

Doctor Fabio jerked and whirled to face the door with a look of utter astonishment on his face. A cabinet behind his desk which had been closed during my first visit was now open. It was a small, gaudy, but functional shrine, a platform for the working of spells. At the moment, it was illuminated by half a dozen candles spaced out around a Seal of Solomon containing two photos—one of Irwin, and one of Doctor Fabio, bound together with a loop of what looked like dark grey yarn.

I could feel the energy stolen from Irwin coursing into the room, into the shrine. From there, I had no doubt, it was being funneled into Doctor Fabio himself. I could sense the intensity of his presence much more sharply than I had that morning, as if he had somehow become more metaphysically massive, filling up more of the room with his presence.

"Hiya, Doc," I said. "You know, it's a pity this place isn't Saint Mark's Academy for the Resourceful and Talented."

He blinked at me. "Uh. What?"

"Because then the place would be S.M.A.R.T. Instead, you're just S.M.A.G.T."

"What?" he said, clearly confused, outraged, and terrified.

"Let me demonstrate," I said, extending my hand. I funneled my will into it and said, "*Smagt!*"

The exact words you use for a spell aren't important, except that they can't be from a language you're too familiar with. Nonsense words are best, generally speaking. Using "smagt" for a combination of naked force and air magic worked just as well as any other word would have. The energy rushed out of me, into the cabinet shrine, and exploded in a blast of kinetic energy and wind. Candles and other decorative objects flew everywhere. Shelves cracked and collapsed.

The spell had been linked to the shrine. It unraveled as I disrupted all the precisely aligned objects that had helped direct and focus its energy. One of the objects had been a small glass bottle of black ink. Most of it wound up splattered on the side of Doctor Fabio's face.

He stood with his jaw slack, half of his face covered in black ink, the other half gone so pale that he resembled a Renaissance Venetian masque.

"Y-you...you..."

"Wizard," I said quietly. "White Council. Heck, Doctor, I'm even a Warden these days."

His face became absolutely bloodless.

"Yeah," I said quietly. "You know us. I'm going to suggest that you answer my questions with extreme cooperation, Doctor. Because we frown on the use of black magic."

"Please," he said, "anything."

"How do you know us?" I asked. The White Council was hardly a secret, but given that most of the world didn't believe in magic, much less wizards, and that the supernatural crowd in general is cautious with sharing information, it was a given that your average Joe would have no idea that the Council even existed—much less that they executed anyone guilty of breaking one of the Laws of Magic.

"V-v-venator," he said. "I was a Venator. One of the Venatori Umbrorum. Retired."

The Hunters in the Shadows. Or of the Shadows, depending on how you read it. They were a boys club made up of the guys who had the savvy to be clued in to the supernatural world, but without the talent it took to be a true wizard. Mostly academic types. They'd been invaluable assets in the White Council's war with the Red Court, gathering information and interfering with our enemy's lines of supply and support. They were old allies of the Council—and any Venator would know the price of violating the Laws.

"A Venator should know better than to dabble in this kind of thing," I said in a very quiet voice. "The answer to this next question could save your life—or end it."

Doctor Fabio licked his lips and nodded, a jerky little motion.

"Why?" I asked him quietly. "Why were you taking essence from the boy?"

"H-he... He had so *much*. I didn't think it would hurt him and I..." He cringed back from me as he spoke the last words. "I... needed to grow some hair."

I blinked my eyes slowly. Twice. "Did you say...hair?"

"Rogaine didn't work!" he all but wailed. "And that transplant surgery wasn't viable for my hair and skin type!" He bowed his head and ran fingertips through his thick head of hair. "Look, see? Look how well it's come in. But if I don't maintain it..."

"You…used black magic. To grow *hair*."

"I…" He looked everywhere but at me. "I tried *everything* else first. I never meant to harm anyone. It never hurt anyone *before*."

"Irwin's a little more dependent on his essence than most," I told him. "You might have killed him."

Fabio's eyes widened in terror. "You mean he's…he's a…"

"Let's just say that his mother is his second scariest parent and leave it at that," I said. I pointed at his chair and said, "Sit."

Fabio sat.

"Do you wish to live?"

"Yes. Yes, I don't want any trouble with the White Council."

Heavy footsteps came pounding up behind us. Steve and his unbloodied buddy appeared in the doorway, carrying their batons. "Doctor Fabio!" Steve cried.

"Don't make me trash your guys," I told Fabio.

"Get out!" Fabio all but screamed at them.

They came to a confused stop. "But…sir?"

"Get out, get out!" Fabio screamed. "Tell the police there's no problem here when they arrive!"

"Sir?"

"Tell them!" Fabio screamed, his voice going up several octaves. "For God's sake, man! Go!"

Steve, and his buddy, went. They looked bewildered, but they went.

"Thank you," I said, when they left. No need to play bad cop at this point. If Fabio got any more scared, he might collapse into jelly. "Do you want to live, Doctor?"

He swallowed. He nodded once.

"Then I suggest you alter your hairstyle to complete baldness," I replied. "Or else learn to accept your receding hairline for what it is—the natural progression of your life. You will discontinue *all* use of magic from this point forward. And I do mean all. If I catch you with so much as a Ouija board or a deck of Tarot cards, I'm going to make you disappear. Do you get me?"

It was a hollow threat. The guy hadn't broken any of the Laws, technically speaking, since Irwin hadn't died. And I had no intention of turning anyone over to the tender mercies of the Wardens if I could possibly avoid it. But this guy clearly had problems recognizing priorities. If he kept going the way he was, he might slide down into true practice of the black arts. Best to scare him away from that right now.

"I understand," he said in a very meek voice.

"Now," I said. "I'm going to go watch over Irwin. You aren't going to interfere. I'll be staying until his mother arrives."

"Are...are you going to tell her what I've done?"

"You bet your ass I am," I said. "And God have mercy on your soul."

Irwin was awake when I got back to the infirmary, and Nurse Jen had just finished stitching closed a cut on the wounded guard's scalp. She'd shaved a big, irregularly shaped section of his hair off to get it done, too, and he looked utterly ridiculous—even more so when she wrapped his entire cranium in bandages to keep the stitches covered.

I went into Irwin's room and said, "How you feeling?"

"Tired," he said. "But better than earlier today."

"Irwin," Nurse Jen said firmly.

"Yes ma'am," Irwin said, and meekly placed the breathing mask over his nose and mouth.

"Your mom's coming to see you," I said.

The kid brightened. "She is? Oh, uh. That's fantastic!" He frowned. "It's not...because of me being sick? Her work is very important."

"Maybe a little," I said. "But mostly, I figure it's because she loves you."

Irwin rolled his eyes but he smiled. "Yeah, well. I guess she's okay. Hey, is there anything else to eat?"

Later, after Irwin had eaten (again), he slept.

"His temperature's back down, and his breathing is clear," Nurse Jen said, shaking her head. "I could have sworn we were going to have to get him to an ICU a few hours ago."

"Kids," I said. "They bounce back fast."

She frowned at Irwin and then at me. Then she said, "It was Fabio, wasn't it. He was doing something."

"Something like what?" I asked.

She shook her head. "I don't know. I just know it…feels like something that's true. He's the one who didn't want you here. He's the one who sent security to run you out just as Irwin got worse."

"You might be right," I said. "And you don't have to worry about it happening again."

She studied me for a moment. Then she said, simply, "Good."

I lifted my eyebrows. "That's one hell of a good sense of intuition you have, nurse."

She snorted. "I'm still not going out with you."

"Story of my life," I said, smiling.

Then I stretched out my legs, settled into my chair, and joined Bigfoot Irwin in dreamland.

Bigfoot on Campus

Takes place between *Turn Coat* and *Changes*

The campus police officer folded his hands and stared at me from across the table. "Coffee?"

"What flavor is it?" I asked.

He was in his forties, a big, solid man with bags under his calm, wary eyes, and his name tag read DEAN. "It's coffee-flavored coffee."

"No mocha?"

"Fuck mocha."

"Thank God," I said. "Black."

Officer Dean gave me hot black coffee in a paper cup, and I sipped at it gratefully. I was almost done shivering. It just came in intermittent bursts now. The old wool blanket Dean had given me was more gesture than cure.

"Am I under arrest?" I asked him.

Officer Dean moved his shoulders in what could have been a shrug. "That's what we're going to talk about."

"Uh-huh," I said.

"Maybe," he said in a slow, rural drawl, "you could explain to me why I found you in the middle of an orgy."

"Well," I said, "if you're going to be in an orgy, the middle is the best spot, isn't it."

He made a thoughtful sound. "Maybe you could explain why there was a car on the fourth floor of the dorm."

"Classic college prank," I said.

He grunted. "Usually when that happens, it hasn't made big holes in the exterior wall."

"Someone was avoiding the cliché?" I asked.

He looked at me for a moment, and said, "What about all the blood?"

"There were no injuries, were there?"

"No," he said.

"Then who cares? Some film student probably watched *Carrie* too many times."

Officer Dean tapped his pencil's eraser on the tabletop. It was the most agitated thing I'd seen him do. "Six separate calls in the past three hours with a Bigfoot sighting on campus. Bigfoot. What do you know about that?"

"Well, kids these days, with their Internets and their video games and their iPods. Who knows what they thought they saw."

Officer Dean put down his pencil. He looked at me, and said, calmly, "My job is to protect a bunch of kids with access to every means of self-destruction known to man from not only the criminal element but themselves. I got chemistry students who can make their own meth, Ecstasy, and LSD. I got ROTC kids with access to automatic weapons and explosives. I got enough alcohol going through here on a weekly basis to float a battleship. I got a thriving trade in recreational drugs. I got lives to protect."

"Sounds tiring."

"About to get tired of you," he said. "Start giving it to me straight."

"Or you'll arrest me?" I asked.

"No," Dean said. "I bounce your face off my knuckles for a while. Then I ask again."

"Isn't that unprofessional conduct?"

"Fuck conduct," Dean said. "I got kids to look after."

I sipped the coffee some more. Now that the shivers had begun to subside, I finally felt the knotted muscles in my belly begin to relax. I slowly settled back into my chair. Dean hadn't blustered or tried to intimidate me in any way. He wasn't trying to scare me into talking. He was just telling me how it was going to be. And he drank his coffee old-school.

I kinda liked the guy.

"You aren't going to believe me," I said.

"I don't much," he said. "Try me."

"Okay," I said. "My name is Harry Dresden. I'm a professional wizard."

Officer Dean pursed his lips. Then he leaned forward slightly and listened.

The client wanted me to meet him at a site in the Ouachita Mountains in eastern Oklahoma. Looking at them, you might not realize they were mountains, they're so old. They've had millions of years of wear and tear on them, and they've been ground down to nubs. The site used to be on an Indian reservation, but they don't call them reservations anymore. They're Tribal Statistical Areas now.

I showed my letter and my ID to a guy in a pickup, who just happened to pull up next to me for a friendly chat at a lonely stop sign on a winding back road. I don't know what the tribe called his office, but I recognized a guardian when I saw one. He read the letter and waved me through in an even friendlier manner than he had used when he approached me. It's nice to be welcomed somewhere, once in a while.

I parked at the spot indicated on the map and hiked a good mile and a half into the hills, taking a heavy backpack with me. I found a pleasant spot to set up camp. The mid-October weather was crisp, but I had a good sleeping bag and would be comfortable as long as it didn't start raining. I dug a fire pit and ringed it in stones, built a modest fire out of fallen limbs, and laid out my sleeping bag on a foam camp pad. By the time it got dark, I was well into preparing the dinner I'd brought with me. The scent of foil-wrapped potatoes baking in coals blended with that of the steaks I had spitted and roasting over the fire.

Can I cook a camp meal or what?

Bigfoot showed up half an hour after sunset.

One minute, I was alone. The next, he simply stepped out into view. He was huge. Not huge like a big person, but huge like a horse, with that same sense of raw animal power and mass. He was nine feet tall at least and probably tipped the scales at well over six hundred pounds. His powerful, wide-shouldered body was covered in long, dark brown hair. Even though he stood in plain sight in my firelight, I could barely see the buckskin bag he had slung over one shoulder and across his chest, the hair was so long.

"Strength of a River in His Shoulders," I said. "You're welcome at my fire."

"Wizard Dresden," River Shoulders rumbled. "It is good to see you." He took a couple of long steps and hunkered down opposite the fire from me. "Man. That smells good."

"Darn right it does," I said. I proceeded with the preparations in companionable silence while River Shoulders stared thoughtfully at the fire. I'd set up my camp this way for a reason—it made me the host and River Shoulders my guest. It meant I was obliged to provide food and drink, and he was obliged to behave with decorum. Guest-and-host relationships are damned near laws of physics in the supernatural world: They almost never get violated, and when they do, it's a big deal. Both of us felt a lot more comfortable around one another this way.

Okay. Maybe it did a wee bit more to make me feel comfortable than it did River Shoulders, but he was a repeat customer, I liked him, and I figured he probably didn't get treated to a decent steak all that often.

We ate the meal in an almost ritualistic silence, too, other than River making some appreciative noises as he chewed. I popped open a couple of bottles of McAnnally's Pale, my favorite brew by a veritable genius of hops, back in Chicago. River liked it so much that he gave me an inquisitive glance when his bottle was empty. So I emptied mine and produced two more.

After that, I filled a pipe with expensive tobacco, lit it, took a few puffs, and passed it to him. He nodded and took it. We smoked and finished our beers. By then, the fire had died down to glowing embers.

"Thank you for coming," River Shoulders rumbled. "Again, I come to seek your help on behalf of my son."

"Third time you've come to me," I said.

"Yes." He rummaged in his pouch and produced a small, heavy object. He flicked it to me. I caught it and squinted at it in the dim light. It was a gold nugget about as big as a Ping-Pong ball. I nodded and tossed it back to him. River Shoulders's brows lowered into a frown.

You have to understand. A frown on a mug like his looked indistinguishable from scowling fury. It turned his eyes into shadowed caves with nothing but a faint gleam showing from far back in them. It made his jaw muscles bunch and swell into knots the size of tennis balls on the sides of his face.

"You will not help him," the Bigfoot said.

I snorted. "*You're* the one who isn't helping him, big guy."

"I am," he said. "I am hiring you."

"You're his *father*," I said quietly. "And he doesn't even know your name. He's a good kid. He deserves more than that. He deserves the truth."

He shook his head slowly. "Look at me. Would he even accept my help?"

"You aren't going to know unless you try it," I said. "And I never said I wouldn't help him."

At that, River Shoulders frowned a little more.

I curbed an instinct to edge away from him.

"Then what do you want in exchange for your services?" he asked.

"I help the kid," I said. "You meet the kid. That's the payment. That's the deal."

"You do not know what you are asking," he said.

"With respect, River Shoulders, this is not a negotiation. If you want my help, I just told you how to get it."

He became very still at that. I got the impression that maybe people didn't often use tactics like that when they dealt with him.

When he spoke, his voice was a quiet, distant rumble. "You have no right to ask this."

"Yeah, um. I'm a wizard. I meddle. It's what we do."

"Manifestly true." He turned his head slightly away. "You do not know how much you ask."

"I know that kid deserves more than you've given him."

"I have seen to his protection. To his education. That is what fathers do."

"Sure," I said. "But you weren't ever *there*. And that *matters*."

Absolute silence fell for a couple of minutes.

"Look," I said gently. "Take it from a guy who knows. Growing up without a dad is terrifying. You're the only father he's ever going to have. You can go hire Superman to look out for Irwin if you want to, and he'd still be the wrong guy—because he isn't you."

River toyed with the empty bottle, rolling it across his enormous fingers like a regular guy might have done with a pencil.

"Do you want me on this?" I asked him. "No hard feelings if you don't."

River looked up at me again and nodded slowly. "I know that if you agree to help him, you will do so. I will pay your price."

"Okay," I said. "Tell me about Irwin's problem."

"What'd he say?" Officer Dean asked.

"He said the kid was at the University of Oklahoma for school," I said. "River'd had a bad dream and knew that the kid's life was in danger."

The cop grunted. "So…Bigfoot is a psychic?"

"Think about it. No one ever gets a good picture of one, much less a clean shot," I said. "Despite all the expeditions and TV shows and whatnot. River's people have got more going for them than being huge and strong. My guess is that they're smarter than humans. Maybe a lot smarter. My guess is they know magic of some kind, too."

"Jesus," Officer Dean said. "You really believe all this, don't you."

"I want to believe," I said. "And I told you that you wouldn't."

Dean grunted. Then he said, "Usually they're too drunk to make sense when I get a story like this. Keep going."

I got to Norman, Oklahoma, a bit before noon the next morning. It was a Wednesday, which was a blessing. In the Midwest, if you show up to a college town on a weekend, you risk running into a football game. In my experience, that resulted in universal problems with traffic, available hotel rooms, and drunken football hooligans.

Or wait: *Soccer* is the one with hooligans. Drunken American football fans are just...drunks, I guess.

River had provided me with a small dossier he'd had prepared, which included a copy of his kid's class schedule. I parked my car in an open spot on the street not too far from campus and ambled on over. I got some looks: I sort of stand out in a crowd. I'm a lot closer to seven feet tall than six, which might be one reason why River Shoulders liked to hire me—I look a lot less tiny than other humans, to him. Add in the big black leather duster and the scar on my face, and I looked like the kind of guy you'd want to avoid in dark alleys.

The university campus was as confusing as all of them are, with buildings that had constantly evolved into and out of multiple roles over the years. They were all named after people I doubt any of the students had ever heard of, or cared about, and there seemed to be no organizational logic at all at work there. It was a pretty enough campus, I supposed. Lots of redbrick and brownstone buildings. Lots of architectural doohickeys on many of the buildings, in a kind of quasi-classical Greek style. The ivy that was growing up many of the walls seemed a little too cultivated and obvious for my taste. Then again, I had exactly the same amount of regard for the Ivy League as I did for the Big 12. The grass was an odd color, like maybe someone had sprayed it with a blue-green dye or something, though I had no idea what kind of delusional creep would do something so pointless.

And, of course, there were students—a whole lot of kids, all of them with things to do and places to be. I could have wandered around all day, but I thought I'd save myself the headache of attempting to apply logic to a university campus and stopped a few times to ask for directions. Irwin Pounder, River Shoulders's son, had a physics course at noon, so I picked up a notebook and a couple of pens at the university bookstore and ambled on into the large classroom. It was a perfect disguise. The notebook was college-ruled.

I sat near the back, where I could see both doors into the room, and waited. Bigfoot Irwin was going to stand out in the crowd almost as badly as I did. The kid was huge. River had shown me a photo that he kept in his medicine bag, carefully laminated to protect it from the elements. Irwin's mom could have been a second-string linebacker for the Bears. Carol Pounder was a formidable woman, and over six feet tall. But her boy was a head taller than she already, and still had the awkward, too-lean look of someone who wasn't finished growing. His shoulders had come in, though, and it looked like he might have had to turn sideways to walk through doors.

I waited and waited, watching both doors, until the professor arrived, and the class started. Irwin never arrived. I was going to leave, but it actually turned out to be kind of interesting. The professor was a lunatic but a really entertaining one. The guy drank liquid nitrogen, right there in front of everybody, and blew it out his nose in this huge jet of vapor. I applauded along with everyone else, and before I knew it, the lecture was over. I might even have learned something.

Okay.

Maybe there were *some* redeeming qualities to a college education.

I went to Irwin's next class, which was a freshman biology course, in another huge classroom.

No Irwin.

He wasn't at his four o'clock math class, either, and I emerged from it bored and cranky. None of Irwin's other teachers held a candle to Dr. Indestructo.

Huh.

Time for plan B.

River's dossier said that Irwin was playing football for OU. He'd made the team as a walk-on, and River had been as proud as any father would be about the athletic prowess of his son. So I ambled on over to the Sooners' practice field, where the team was warming up with a run.

Even among the football players, Irwin stood out. He was half a head taller than any of them, at least my own height. He looked gangly and thin beside the fellows around him, even with the shoulder pads on, but I recognized his face. I'd last seen him when he was about fourteen. Though his rather homely features had changed a bit, they seemed stronger, and more defined. There was no mistaking his dark, intelligent eyes.

I stuck my hands in the pockets of my old leather duster and waited, watching the field. I'd found the kid, and, absent any particular danger, I was in no particular hurry. There was no sense in charging into the middle of Irwin's football practice and his life and disrupting everything. I'm just not that kind of guy.

Okay, well.

I try not to be.

"Seems to keep happening, though, doesn't it," I said to myself. "You show up on somebody's radar, and things go to DEFCON 1 a few minutes later."

"I'm sorry?" said a young woman's voice.

"Ah," said Officer Dean. "This is where the girl comes in."

"Who said there was a girl?"

"There's always a girl."

"Well," I said, "yes and no."

She was blond, about five-foot-six, and my logical mind told me that every inch of her was a bad idea. The rest of me, especially my hindbrain, suggested that she would be an ideal mate. Preferably sooner rather than later.

There was nothing in particular about her that should have caused my hormones to rage. I mean, she was young and fit, and she had the body of the young and fit, and that's hardly ever unpleasant to look at. She had eyes the color of cornflowers and rosy cheeks, and she was a couple of notches above cute, when it came to her face. She was wearing running shorts, and her legs were smooth and generally excellent.

Some women just have it. And no, I can't tell you what "it" means because I don't get it myself. It was something mindless, something chemical, and even as my metaphorically burned fingers were telling me to walk away, the rest of me was going through that male physiological response the science guys in the Netherlands have documented recently.

Not *that* one.

Well, maybe a little.

I'm talking about the response where when a pretty girl is around, it hits the male brain like a drug and temporarily impairs his cognitive function, literally dropping the male IQ.

And hey, how Freudian is it that the study was conducted in the Netherlands?

This girl dropped that IQ-nuke on my brain, and I was standing there staring a second later while she smiled uncertainly at me.

"Um, sorry?" I asked. "My mind was in the Netherlands."

Her dimple deepened, and her eyes sparkled. She knew all about the brain nuke. "I just said that you sounded like a dangerous guy." She winked at me. It was adorable. "I like those."

"You're, uh. You're into bad boys, eh?"

"Maybe," she said, lowering her voice and drawing the word out a little, as if it was a confession. She spoke with a very faint drawl. "Plus, I like meeting new people from all kinds of places, and you don't exactly strike me as a local, darlin'."

"You dig dangerous guys who are just passing through," I said. "Do you ever watch those cop shows on TV?"

She tilted back her head and laughed. "Most boys don't give me lip like that in the first few minutes of conversation."

"I'm not a boy," I said.

She gave me a once-over with those pretty eyes, taking a heartbeat longer about it than she really needed. "No," she said. "No, you are not."

My inner nonmoron kept on stubbornly ringing alarm bells, and the rest of me slowly became aware of them. My glands thought that I'd better keep playing along. It was the only way to find out what the girl might have been interested in, right? Right. I was absolutely not continuing the conversation because I had gone soft in the head.

"I hope that's not a problem," I said.

"I just don't see how it could be. I'm Connie."

"Harry."

"So what brings you to Norman, Harry?"

"Taking a look at a player," I said.

Her eyes brightened. "Ooooo. You're a scout?"

"Maybe," I said, in the same tone she'd used earlier.

Connie laughed again. "I'll bet you talk to silly college girls like me all the time."

"Like you?" I replied. "No, not so much."

Her eyes sparkled again. "You may have found my weakness. I'm the kind of girl who likes a little flattery."

"And here I was thinking you liked something completely different."

She covered her mouth with one hand, and her cheeks got a little pinker. "Harry. That's not how one talks to young ladies in the South."

"Obviously. I mean, you look so outraged. Should I apologize?"

"Oh," she said, her smile widening. "I just *have* to collect you." Connie's eyes sparkled again, and I finally got it.

Her eyes weren't *twinkling.*

They were becoming increasingly flecked with motes of molten silver.

Cutie-pie was a frigging vampire.

I've worked for years on my poker face. Years. It still sucks pretty bad, but I've been working on it. So I'm sure my smile was only slightly wooden when I asked, "Collect me?"

I might not have been hiding my realization very well, but either Connie was better at poker than me, or else she really was too absorbed in the conversation to notice. "Collect you," she said. "When I meet someone worthwhile, I like to have dinner with them. And we'll talk and tell stories and laugh, and I'll get a picture and put it in my memory book."

"Um," I said. "Maybe you're a little young for me."

She threw back her head and gave a full-throated laugh. "Oh, Harry. I'm talking about sharing a meal. That's all, honestly. I know I'm a terrible flirt, but I didn't think you were taking me seriously."

I watched her closely as she spoke, searching for the predatory calculation that I knew had to be in there. Vampires of the White Court—

"Wait," Dean said. "Vampires of the White Castle?"

I sighed. "White Court."

Dean grunted. "Why not just call her a vampire?"

"They come in a lot of flavors," I said.

"And this one was vanilla?"

"There's no such thing as..." I rubbed at the bridge of my nose. "Yes."

Dean nodded. "So why not just call 'em vanilla vampires?"

"I'll...bring it up at the next wizard meeting," I said.

"So the vampire is where all the blood came from?"

"No." I sighed. "This kind doesn't feed on blood."

"No? What do they eat, then?"

"Life-energy."

"Huh?"

I sighed again. "Sex."

"Finally, the story gets good. So they *eat* sex?"

"Life-energy," I repeated. "The sex is just how they get started."

"Like sticking fangs into your neck," Dean said. "Only instead of fangs, I guess they use—"

"Look, do you want the story or not?"

Dean leaned back in his chair and propped his feet up on his desk. "You kidding? This is the best one in years."

Anyway, I watched Connie closely, but I saw no evidence of anything in her that I knew had to be there. Vampires are predators who hunt the most dangerous game on the planet. They generally aren't shy about it, either. They don't really need to be. If a White Court vampire wants to feed off a human, all she really has to do is crook her finger, and he comes running. There isn't any ominous music. Nobody sparkles. As far as anyone looking on is concerned, a girl winks at a boy and goes off somewhere to make out. Happens every day.

They don't get all coy asking you out to dinner, and they sure as hell don't have pictures in a memory book.

This was weird, and long experience has taught me that when the unexplained is bouncing around right in front of you, the smart thing is to back off and figure out what the hell is going on. In my line of work, what you don't know can kill you.

But I didn't get the chance. There was a sharp whistle from a coach somewhere on the field, and football players came rumbling off it. One of them came loping toward us, put a hand on top of the six-foot chain-link fence, and vaulted it in one easy motion. Bigfoot Irwin landed lightly, grinning, and continued directly toward Connie.

She let out a girlish squeal of delight and pounced on him. He caught her. She wrapped her legs around his hips, held his face in her hands, and kissed him thoroughly. They came up for air a moment later.

"Irwin," she said, "I met someone interesting. Can I collect him?"

The kid only had eyes for Connie. Not that I could blame him, really. His voice was a basso rumble, startlingly like River Shoulders's. "I'm always in favor of dinner at the Brewery."

She dismounted and beamed at him. "Good. Irwin, this is..."

The kid finally looked up at me and blinked. "Harry."

"Heya, Irwin," I said. "How're things?"

Connie looked back and forth between us. "You *know* each other?"

"He's a friend," Irwin said.

"Dinner," Connie declared. "Harry, say you'll share a meal with me."

Interesting choice of words, all things considered.

I think I had an idea what had caused River's bad dream. If a vampire had attached herself to Irwin, the kid was in trouble. Given the addictive nature of Connie's attentions, and the degree of control it could give her over Irwin…maybe he wasn't the only one who could be in trouble.

My, how little Irwin had grown. I wondered exactly how much of his father's supernatural strength he had inherited. He looked like he could break me in half without causing a blip in his heart rate. He and Connie looked at me with hopeful smiles, and I suddenly felt like maybe I was the crazy one. Expressions like that should not inspire worry, but every instinct I had told me that something wasn't right.

My smile probably got even more wooden. "Sure," I said. "Why not?"

The Brewery was a lot like every other sports bar you'd find in college towns, with the possible exception that it actually was a brewery. Small and medium-sized tanks stood here and there throughout the place, with signs on each describing the kind of beer that was under way. Apparently, the beer sampler was traditional. I made polite noises when I tried each, but they were unexceptional. Okay, granted I was probably spoiled by having Mac's brew available back at home. It wasn't the Brewery's fault that their brews were merely excellent. Mac's stuff was epic, it was legend. Tough to measure up to that.

I kept one hand under the table, near a number of tools I thought I might need, all the way through the meal, and waited for the other shoe to drop—only it never did. Connie and Irwin chattered away like any young couple, snuggled up to one another on adjacent chairs. The girl was charming, funny, and a playful flirt, but Irwin didn't seem discomfited by it. I kept my responses restrained anyway. I didn't want to find out a couple of seconds too late that the seemingly innocent banter was how Connie got her psychic hooks into me.

But a couple of hours went by, and nothing.

"Irwin's never told me anything about his father," Connie said.

"I don't know much," Irwin said. "He's...kept his distance over the years. I've looked for him a couple of times, but I never wanted to push him."

"How mysterious," Connie said.

I nodded. "For someone like him, I think the word 'eccentric' might apply better."

"He's rich?" Connie asked.

"I feel comfortable saying that money isn't one of his concerns," I said.

"I knew it!" Connie said, and looked slyly at Irwin. "There had to be a reason. I'm only into you for your money."

Instead of answering, Irwin calmly picked Connie up out of her chair, using just the muscles of his shoulders and arms, and deposited her on his lap. "Sure you are."

Connie made a little groaning sound and bit her lower lip. "God. I know it's not PC, but I've got to say—I am *into* it when you get all caveman on me, Pounder."

"I know." Irwin kissed the tip of her nose and turned to me. "So, Harry. What brings you to Norman?"

"I was passing through," I said easily. "Your dad asked me to look in on you."

"Just casually," Irwin said, his dark eyes probing. "Because he's such a casual guy."

"Something like that," I said.

"Not that I mind seeing you," Irwin said, "but in case you missed it, I'm all grown-up now. I don't need a babysitter. Even a cool, expensive one."

"If you did, my rates are very reasonable," Connie said.

"We'll talk," Irwin replied, sliding his arms around her waist. The girl wasn't exactly a junior petite, but she looked tiny on Irwin's scale. She hopped up, and said, "I'm going to go make sure there isn't barbecue sauce on my nose, and then we can take the picture. Okay?"

"Sure," Irwin said, smiling. "Go."

Once she was gone from sight, Irwin looked at me and dropped his smile. "Okay," he said resignedly. "What does he want this time?"

There wasn't loads of time, so I didn't get all coy with the subject matter. "He's worried about you. He thinks you may be in danger."

Irwin arched his eyebrows. "From what?"

I just looked at him.

His expression suddenly turned into a scowl, and the air around grew absolutely thick with energy that seethed for a point of discharge. "Wait. This is about Connie?"

I couldn't answer him for a second, the air felt so close. The last time I'd felt this much latent, waiting power, I'd been standing next to my old mentor, Ebenezar McCoy, when he was gathering his strength for a spell.

That pretty much answered my questions about River Shoulders's people having access to magical power. The kid was a freaking dynamo of it. I had to be careful. I didn't want to be the guy who was unlucky enough to ground out that storm cloud of waiting power. So I answered Irwin cautiously and calmly.

"I'm not sure yet. But I know for a fact that she's not exactly what she seems to be."

His nostrils flared, and I saw him make an effort to remain collected. His voice was fairly even. "Meaning what?"

"Meaning I'm not sure yet," I said.

"So what? You're going to hang around here butting into my life?"

I held up both hands. "It isn't like that."

"It's just like that," Irwin said. "My dad spends my whole life anywhere else but here, and now he thinks he can just decide when to intrude on it?"

"Irwin," I said, "I'm not here to try to make you do anything. He asked me to look in on you. I promised I would. And that's all."

He scowled for a moment, then smoothed that expression away. "No sense in being mad at the messenger, I guess," he said. "What do you mean about Connie?"

"She's..." I faltered, there. You don't just sit down with a guy and tell him, "Hey, your girlfriend is a vampire, could you pass the ketchup?" I sighed. "Look, Irwin. Everybody sees the world a certain way. And we all kind of...well, we all sort of decide together what's real and what isn't real, right?"

"Magic's real," Irwin said impatiently. "Monsters are real. Supernatural stuff actually exists. You're a professional wizard."

I blinked at him, several times.

"What?" he asked, and smiled gently. "Don't let the brow ridge fool you. I'm not an idiot, man. You think you can walk into my life the way you have, twice, and not leave me with an itch to scratch? You made me ask questions. I went and got answers."

"Uh. How?" I asked.

"Wasn't hard. There's an Internet. And this organization called the 'Paranet' of all the cockamamie things, that got started a few years ago. Took me like ten minutes to find it online and start reading through their message boards. I can't believe everyone in the world doesn't see this stuff. It's not like anyone is trying very hard to keep it secret."

"People don't want to know the truth," I said. "That makes it simple to hide. Wow, ten minutes? Really? I guess I'm not really an Internetty person."

"Internetty," Irwin said, seriously. "I guess you aren't."

I waved a hand. "Irwin, you need to know this. Connie isn't—"

The pretty vampire plopped herself back down into Irwin's lap and kissed his cheek. "Isn't what?"

"The kind to stray," I said, smoothly. "I was just telling Irwin how much I'd like to steal you away from him, but I figure you're the sort who doesn't play that kind of game."

"True enough," she agreed cheerfully. "I know where I want to sleep tonight." Maybe it was unconscious, the way she wriggled when she said it, but Irwin's eyes got a slightly glazed look to them.

I remembered being that age. A girl like Connie would have been a mind-numbing distraction to me back then even if she hadn't been a vampire. And Irwin was clearly in love, or as close to it as he could manage through the haze of hormones surrounding him. Reasoning with him wasn't going to accomplish anything—unless I made him angry. Passion is a huge force when you're Irwin's age, and I'd taken enough beatings for one lifetime. I'd never be able to explain the danger to him. He just didn't have a frame of reference...

He just didn't know.

I stared at Connie for a second with my mouth open.

"What?" she asked.

"You don't know," I said.

"Know what?" she asked.

"You don't know that you're..." I shook my head, and said to Irwin, "She doesn't *know*."

"Hang on," Dean said. "Why is that significant?"

"Vampires are just like people until the first time they feed," I said. "Connie didn't know that bad things would happen when she did."

"What kinda bad things?"

"The first time they feed, they don't really know it's coming. They have no control over it, no restraint—and whoever they feed on dies as a result."

"So she was the threat that Bigfoot dreamed about?"

"I'm getting to it."

Irwin's expression had darkened again, into a glower almost exactly like River Shoulders's, and he stood up.

Connie was frowning at me as she was abruptly displaced. "Don't know wh—oof, Pounder!"

"We're done," Irwin said to me. His voice wasn't exactly threatening, but it was absolutely certain, and his leashed anger all but made the air crackle. "Nice to see you again, Harry. Tell my dad to call. Or write. Or do anything but try to tell me how to live my life."

Connie blinked at him. "Wait...wait, what's wrong?"

Irwin left a few twenties on the table, and said, "We're going."

"What? What happened?"

"We're *going*," Irwin said. This time, he did sound a little angry.

Connie's bewilderment suddenly shifted into some flavor of outrage. She narrowed her lovely eyes, and snapped, "I am not your pet, Pounder."

"I'm not trying to..." Irwin took a slow, deep breath, and said, more calmly, "I'm upset. I need some space. I'll explain when I calm down. But we need to go."

She folded her arms, and said, "Go calm down, then. But I'm not going to be rude to our guest."

Irwin looked at me, and said, "We going to have a problem?"

Wow. The kid had learned a lot about the world since the last time I'd seen him. He recognized that I wasn't a playful puppy dog. He realized that if I'd been sent to protect him, and I thought Connie was a threat, that I might do something about it. And he'd just told me that if I did, he was going to object. Strenuously. No protests, no threats, just letting me know that he knew the score and was willing to do something about it if I made him. The guys who are seriously capable handle themselves like that.

"No problem," I said, and made it a promise. "If I think something needs to be done, we'll talk first."

The set of his shoulders eased, and he nodded at me. Then he turned and stalked out. People watched him go, warily.

Connie shook her head slowly, and asked, "What did you say?"

"Um," I said. "I think he feels like his dad is intruding on his life."

"You don't say." She shook her head. "That's not your fault. He's usually so collected. Why is he acting like such a jerk?"

"Issues," I said, shrugging. "Everyone has a parental issue or two."

"Still. It's beneath him to behave that way." She shook her head. "Sometimes he makes me want to slap him. But I'd need to get a chair to stand on."

"I don't take it personally," I assured her. "Don't worry."

"It was about me," she said quietly. "Wasn't it? It's about something I don't know."

"Um," I said.

It was just possible that maybe I'd made a bad call when I decided to meddle between River and his kid. It wasn't my place to shake the pillars of Irwin's life. Or Connie's, for that matter. It was going to be hard enough on her to find out about her supernatural heritage. She didn't need to have the news broken to her by a stranger, on top of that. You'd think that, after years as a professional, I'd know enough to just take River's money, help out his kid, and call it a night.

"Maybe we should walk?" I suggested.

"Sure."

We left and started walking the streets of downtown Norman. The place was alive and growing, like a lot of college towns: plenty of old buildings, some railroad tracks, lots of cracks in the asphalt and the sidewalks. The shops and restaurants had that improvised look that a business district gets when it outlives its original intended purpose and subsequent generations of enterprise take over the space.

We walked in silence for several moments, until Connie finally said, "He's not an angry person. He's usually so calm. But when something finally gets to him..."

"It's hard for him," I said. "He's huge and he's very strong and he knows it. If he loses control of himself, someone could get hurt. He doesn't like the thought of that. So when he starts feeling angry, it makes him tense. Afraid. He's more upset about the fact that he feels so angry than about anything I said or did."

Connie looked up at me pensively for a long moment. Then she said, "Most people wouldn't realize that."

I shrugged.

"What don't I know?" she asked.

I shook my head. "I'm not sure it's my place to tell you."

"But it's about me."

"Yeah."

She smiled faintly. "Then shouldn't I be the one who gets to decide?"

I thought about that one for a moment. "Connie...you're mostly right. But...some things, once said, can't be unsaid. Let me think about it."

She didn't answer.

The silence made me uncomfortable. I tried to chat my way clear of it. "How'd you meet Irwin?"

The question, or maybe the subject matter, seemed to relax her a little. "In a closet at a party. Someone spiked the punch. Neither of us had ever been drunk before, and..." Her cheeks turned a little pink. "And he's just so damned sexy."

"Lot of people wouldn't think so," I noted.

She waved a hand. "He's not pretty. I know that. It's not about that. There's...this energy in him. It's chemical. Assurance. Power. Not just muscles—it's who he is." Her cheeks turned a little pink. "It wasn't exactly love at first sight, I guess. But once the hangover cleared up, that happened, too."

"So you love him?" I asked.

Her smile widened, and her eyes shone the way a young woman's eyes ought to shine. She spoke with calm, simple certainty. "He's the one."

About twenty things to say leapt to my mind. I was going to say something about how she was too young to make that kind of decision. I thought about how she hadn't been out on her own for very long, and how she had no idea where her relationship with Irwin was going to lead. I was going to tell her that only time could tell her if she and Irwin were good for one another and ready to be together, to make that kind of decision. I could have said something about how she needed to stop and think, not make blanket statements about her emotions and the future.

That was when I realized that everything I would have said was something I would have said to a young woman in love—not to a vampire. Not only that, but I heard something in her voice or saw something in her face that told me that my aged wisdom was, at least in this case, dead wrong. My instincts were telling me something that my rational brain had missed.

The kids had something real. I mean, maybe it hadn't gotten off on the most pure and virtuous foot, but that wasn't anything lethal in a relationship. The way they related to one another now? There was a connection there. You could imagine saying their names as a unit, and it *fit*: ConnieandIrwin. Maybe they had some growing to do, but what they had was real.

Not that it mattered. Being in love didn't change the facts. First, that Connie was a vampire. Second, that vampires had to feed. Third, they fed upon their lovers.

"Hold on," Dean said. "You missed something."

"Eh?"

"Girl's a vampire, right?"

"Yeah.

"So," Dean said. "She met the kid in a closet at a party. They already got it on. She done had her first time."

I frowned. "Yeah."

"So how come Kid Bigfoot wasn't dead?"

I nodded. "Exactly. It bothered me, too."

The girl was in love with Irwin, and it meant she was dangerous to him. Hell, she was dangerous to almost everyone. She wasn't even entirely *human*. How could I possibly spring something that big on her?

At the same time, how could I *not*?

"I should have taken the gold," I muttered to myself.

"What?" she asked.

That was when the Town Car pulled up to the curb a few feet ahead of us. Two men got out of the front seat. They wore expensive suits and had thick necks. One of them hadn't had his suit fitted properly—I could see the slight bulge of a sidearm in a shoulder holster. That one stood on the sidewalk and stared at me, his hands clasped in front of him. The driver went around to the rear passenger door and opened it.

"Oh," Connie said. "Marvelous. This is all I need."

"Who is that?" I asked.

"My father."

The man who got out of the back of the limo wore a pearl gray suit that made his thugs' outfits look like secondhand clothing. He was slim, a bit over six feet tall, and his haircut probably cost him more than I made in a week. His hair was dark, with a single swath of silver at each temple, and his skin was weathered and deeply tanned. He wore rings on most of his manicured fingers, all of them sporting large stones.

"Hi, Daddy," Connie said, smiling. She sounded pleasant enough, but she'd turned herself very slightly away from the man as she spoke. A rule of thumb for reading body language is that almost no one can totally hide physical reflections of their state of mind. They can only minimize the signs of it in their posture and movements. If you mentally exaggerate and magnify their body language, it tells you something about what they're thinking.

Connie clearly didn't want to talk to this man. She was ready to flee from her own father should it become necessary. It told me something about the guy. I was almost sure I wasn't going to like him.

He approached the girl, smiling, and after a microhesitation, they exchanged a brief hug. It didn't look like something they'd practiced much.

"Connie," the man said, smiling. He had the same mild drawl his daughter did. He tilted his head to one side and regarded her thoughtfully. "You went blond. It's...charming."

"Thank you, Daddy," Connie said. She was smiling, too. Neither one of them looked sincere to me. "I didn't know you were in town. If you'd called, we could have made an evening of it."

"Spur-of-the-moment thing," he said easily. "I hope you don't mind."

"No, of course not."

Both of them were lying. Parental issues indeed.

"How's that boy you'd taken up with? Irving."

"Irwin," Connie said in a poisonously pleasant tone. "He's great. Maybe even better than that."

He frowned at that, and said, "I see. But he's not here?"

"He had homework tonight," Connie lied.

That drew a small, sly smile out of the man. "I see. Who's your friend?" he asked pleasantly, without actually looking at me.

"Oh," Connie said. "Harry, this is my father, Charles Barrowill. Daddy, this is Harry Dresden."

"Hi," I said brightly.

Barrowill's eyes narrowed to sudden slits, and he took a short, hard breath as he looked at me. He then flicked his eyes left and right around him, as if looking for a good place to dive or maybe a hostage to seize.

"What a pleasure, Mr. Dresden," he said, his voice suddenly tight. "What brings you out to Oklahoma?"

"I heard it was a nice place for perambulating," I said. Behind Barrowill, his guards had picked up on the tension. Both of them had become very still. Barrowill was quiet for a moment, as if trying to parse some kind of meaning from my words. Heavy seconds ticked by, like the quiet before a shootout in an old Western.

A tumbleweed went rolling by in the street. I'm not even kidding. An actual, literal tumbleweed. Man, Oklahoma.

Then Barrowill took a slow breath and said to Connie, "Darling, I'd like to speak to you for a few moments, if you have time."

"Actually…" Connie began.

"Now, please," Barrowill said. There was something ugly under the surface of his pleasant tone. "The car. I'll give you a ride back to the dorms."

Connie folded her arms and scowled. "I'm entertaining someone from out of town, Daddy. I can't just leave him here."

One of the guard's hands twitched.

"Don't be difficult, Connie," Barrowill said. "I don't want to make a scene."

His eyes never left me as he spoke, and I got his message loud and clear. He was taking the girl with him, and he was willing to make things get messy if I tried to stop him.

"It's okay, Connie," I said. "I've been to Norman before. I can find my way to a hotel easily enough."

"You're sure?" Connie asked.

"Definitely."

"Herman," Barrowill said.

The driver opened the passenger door again and stood next to it attentively. He kept his eyes on me, and one hand dangled, clearly ready to go for his gun.

Connie looked back and forth between me and her father for a moment, then sighed audibly and walked over to the car. She slid in, and Herman closed the door behind her.

"I recognize you," I said pleasantly to Barrowill. "You were at the Raith Deeps when Skavis and Malvora tried to pull off their coup. Front row, all the way on one end in the Raith cheering section."

"You have an excellent memory," Barrowill said.

"Got out in one piece, did you?"

The vampire smiled without humor. "What are you doing with my daughter?"

"Taking a walk," I said. "Talking."

"You have nothing to say to her. In the interests of peace between the Court and the Council, I'm willing to ignore this intrusion into my territory. Go in peace. Right now."

"You never told her, did you?" I asked. "Never told her what she was."

One of his jaw muscles twitched. "It is not our way."

"Nah," I said. "You wait until the first time they get twitterpated, experiment with sex, and kill whoever it is they're with. Little harsh on the kids, isn't it?"

"Connie is not some mortal cow. She is a vampire. The initiation builds character she will need to survive and prosper."

"If it was good enough for you, it's good enough for her?"

"Mortal," Barrowill said, "you simply cannot understand. I am her father. It is my obligation to prepare her for her life. The initiation is something she needs."

I lifted my eyebrows. "Holy...that's what happened, isn't it? You sent her off to school to boink some poor kid to death. Hell, I'd bet you had the punch spiked at that party. Except the kid didn't die—so now you're in town to figure out what the hell went wrong."

Barrowill's eyes darkened, and he shook his head. "This is no business of yours. Leave."

"See, that's the thing," I said. "It *is* my business. My client is worried about his kid."

Barrowill narrowed his eyes again. "Irving."

"Irwin," I corrected him.

"Go back to Chicago, wizard," he said. "You're in my territory now."

"This isn't a smart move for you," I said. "The kid's connected. If anything bad happens to him, you're in for trouble."

"Is that a threat?" he asked.

I shook my head. "Chuck, I've got no objection to working things out peaceably. And I've got no objection to doing it the other way. If you know my reputation, then you know what a sincere guy I am."

"Perhaps I should kill you now."

"Here, in public?" I asked. "All these witnesses? You aren't going to do that."

"No?"

"No. Even if you win, you lose. You're just hoping to scare me off." I nodded toward his goons. "Ghouls, right? It's going to take more than two, Chuck. Hell, I like fighting ghouls. No matter what I do to them, I never feel bad about it afterward."

Barrowill missed the reference, like the monsters usually do. He looked at me, then at his Rolex. "I'll give you until midnight to leave the state. After that, you're gone. One way or another."

"Hang on," I said, "I'm terrified. Let me catch my breath."

Barrowill's eyes shifted color slightly, from a deep green to a much paler, angrier shade of green-gold. "I react poorly to those who threaten my family's well-being, Dresden."

"Yeah. You're a regular Ozzie Nelson. John Walton. Ben Cartwright."

"Excuse me?"

"Mr. Drummond? Charles...in Charge? No?"

"What are you blabbering about?"

"Hell's bells, man. Don't any of you White Court bozos ever watch television? I'm giving you pop reference gold, here. Gold."

Barrowill stared at me with opaque, reptilian eyes. Then he said, simply, "Midnight." He took two steps back before he turned his back on me and got into his car. His goons both gave me hard looks before they, too, got into the car and pulled away.

I watched the car roll out. Despite the attitude I'd given Barrowill, I knew better than to take him lightly. Any vampire is a dangerous foe—and one of them with holdings and resources and his own personal brute squad was more so. Not only that but...from his point of view, I was messing around with his little girl's best interests. The vampires of the White Court were, to a degree, as dangerous as they were because they were partly human. They had human emotions, human motivations, human reactions. Barrowill could be as irrationally protective of his family as anyone else.

Except that they were also *inhuman*. All of those human drives were intertwined with a parasitic spirit they called a Hunger, where all the power and hunger of their vampire parts came from.

Take one part human faults and insecurities and add it to one part inhuman power and motivation. What do you get?

Trouble.

"Barrowill?" Officer Dean asked me. "The oil guy? He keeps a stable. Of congressmen."

"Yeah, probably the same guy," I said. "All vampires like having money and status. It makes their lives easier."

Dean snorted. "Every vampire. And every nonvampire."

"*Heh*," I said. "Point."

"You were in a fix," he said. "Tell the girl, you might wreck her. Don't tell her, and you might wreck her and Kid Bigfoot both. Either way, somebody's dad has a bone to pick with you."

"Pretty much."

"Seems to me a smart guy would have washed his hands of the whole mess and left town."

I shrugged. "Yeah. But I was the only guy there."

Forest isn't exactly the dominant terrain in Norman, but there are a few trees, here and there. The point where I'd agreed to meet with River Shoulders was in the center of the Oliver Wildlife Preserve, which was a stand of woods that had been donated to the university for research purposes. As I hiked out into the little wood, it occurred to me that meeting River Shoulders there was like rendezvousing with Jaws in a kiddy wading pool—but he'd picked the spot, so whatever floated the big guy's boat.

It was dark out, and I drew my silver pentacle amulet off my neck to use for light. A whisper of will and a muttered word, and the little symbol glowed with a dim blue light that would let me walk without bumping into a tree. It took me maybe five minutes to get to approximately the right area, and River Shoulders's soft murmur of greeting came to me out of the dark.

We sat down together on a fallen tree, and I told him what I'd learned.

He sat in silence for maybe two minutes after I finished. Then he said, "My son has joined himself to a parasite."

I felt a flash of mild outrage. "You could think of it that way," I said.

"What other way is there?"

"That he's joined himself to a girl. The parasite just came along for the ride."

River Shoulders exhaled a huge breath. It sounded like those pneumatic machines they use to elevate cars at the repair shop. "I see. In your view, the girl is not dangerous. She is innocent."

"She's both," I said. "She can't help being born what she is, any more than you or I."

River Shoulders grunted.

"Have your people encountered the White Court before?"

He grunted again.

"Because the last time I helped Irwin out...I remember being struck by the power of his aura when he was only fourteen. A long-term draining spell that should have killed him only left him sleepy." I eyed him. "But I don't feel anything around you. Stands to reason, your aura would be an order of magnitude greater than your kid's. That's why you've been careful never to touch me. You're keeping your power hidden from me, aren't you?"

"Maybe."

I snorted. "Just the kind of answer I'd expect from a wizard."

"It is not something we care for outsiders to know," he said. "And we are not wizards. We see things differently than mortals. You people are dangerous."

"Heh," I said, and glanced up at his massive form beside mine. "Between the two of us, I'm the dangerous one."

"Like a child waving around his father's gun," River Shoulders said. Something in his voice became gentler. "Though some of you are better than others about it, I admit."

"My point is," I said, "the kid's got a life force like few I've seen. When Connie's Hunger awakened, she fed on him without any kind of restraint, and he wound up with nothing worse than a hangover. Could be that he could handle a life with her just fine."

River Shoulders nodded slowly. His expression might have been thoughtful. It was too dark, and his features too blunt and chiseled to be sure.

"The girl seems genuinely fond of him. And he of her. I mean, I'm not an expert in these things, but they seem to like each other, and even when they have a difference of opinions, they fight fair. That's a good sign." I squinted at him. "Do you really think he's in danger?"

"Yes," River Shoulders said. "They have to kill him now."

I blinked. "What?"

"This...creature. This Barrowill."

"Yeah?"

"It sent its child to this place with the intention that she meet a young man and feed upon him and unknowingly kill him."

"Yeah."

River Shoulders shook his huge head sadly. "What kind of monster does that to its children?"

"Vampires," I said. "It isn't uncommon, from what I hear."

"Because they hurt," River Shoulders said. "Barrowill remembers his own first lover. He remembers being with her. He remembers her death. And his wendigo has had its hand on his heart ever since. It shaped his life."

"Wendigo?"

River Shoulders waved a hand. "General term. Spirit of hunger. Can't ever be sated."

"Ah, gotcha."

"Now, Barrowill. He had his father tell him that this was how it had to be. That it had to be that way to make him a good vampire. So this thing that turned him into a murdering monster is actually a good thing. He spends his whole life trying to convince himself of that." River nodded slowly. "What happens when his child does something differently?"

I felt like a moron. "It means that what his father told him was a lie. It means that maybe he didn't have to be like he is. It means that he's been lying to himself. About everything."

River Shoulders spread his hands, palm up, as if presenting the fact. "That kind of father has to make his children in his own image. He has to make the lie true."

"He has to make sure Connie kills Irwin," I said. "We've got to get him out of there. Maybe both of them."

"How?" River Shoulders said. "She doesn't know. He only knows a little. Neither knows enough to be wise enough to run."

"They shouldn't *have* to run," I growled.

"Avoiding a fight is always better than not avoiding one."

"Disagree," I said. "Some fights *should* be sought out. And fought. And won."

River Shoulders shook his head. "Your father's gun." I sensed a deep current of resistance in River Shoulders on this subject—one that I would never be able to bridge, I suspected. River just wasn't a fighter. "Would you agree it was wisest if they both fled?"

"In this case...it might, yeah. But I think it would only delay the confrontation. Guys like Barrowill have long arms. If he obsesses over it, he'll find them sooner or later."

"I have no right to take his child from him," River Shoulders said. "I am only interested in Irwin."

"Well, I'm not going to be able to separate them," I said. "Irwin nearly started swinging at me when I went anywhere close to that subject." I paused, then added, "But he might listen to you."

River Shoulders shook his head. "He's right. I got no right to walk in and smash his life to splinters after being so far away so long. He'd never listen to me. He's got a lot of anger in him. Maybe for good reasons."

"You're his father," I said. "That might carry more weight than you think."

"I should not have involved you in this," he said. "I apologize for that, wizard. You should go. Let me sort this out on my own."

I eyed River Shoulders.

The big guy was powerful, sure, but he was also slow. He took his time making decisions. He played things out with enormous patience. He was clearly ambivalent over what kind of involvement he should have with his son. It might take him months of observation and cogitation to make a choice.

Most of us don't live that way. I was sure Barrowill didn't. If the vampire was moving, he might be moving now. Like, right now.

"In this particular instance, River Shoulders, you are not thinking clearly," I said. "Action must be taken soon. Preferably tonight."

"I will be what I am," River said firmly.

I stood up from the log and nodded. "Okay," I said. "Me too."

I put in a call to my fellow Warden, "Wild Bill" Meyers, in Dallas, but got an answering service. I left a message that I was in Norman and needed his help, but I had little faith that he'd show up in time. The real downside to being a wizard is that we void the warrantees of anything technological every time we sneeze. Cell phones are worse than useless in our hands, and it makes communications a challenge at times though that was far from the only possible obstacle. If Bill was in, he'd have picked up his phone. He had a big area for his beat and likely had problems of his own—but since Dallas was only three hours away (assuming his car didn't break down), I could hold out hope that he might roll in by morning.

So I got in my busted-up old Volkswagen, picked up a prop, and drove up to the campus alone. I parked somewhere where

I would probably get a ticket. I planned to ignore it. Anarchists have a much easier time finding parking spots.

I got out and walked toward one of the smaller dorm buildings on campus. I didn't have my wizard's staff with me, on account of how weird it looked to walk around with one, but my blasting rod was hanging from its tie inside my leather duster. I doubted I would need it, but better to have it and not need it than the other way around. I got my prop and trudged across a short bit of turquoise-tinted grass to the honors dorms, where Irwin lived. They were tiny, for that campus, maybe five stories, with the building laid out in four right-angled halls, like a plus sign. The door was locked. There's always that kind of security in a dorm building, these days.

I rapped on the glass with my knuckles until a passing student noticed. I held up a cardboard box from the local Pizza 'Spress, and tried to look like I needed a break. I needn't have tried so hard. The kid's eyes were bloodshot and glassy. He was baked on something. He opened the door for me without blinking.

"Thanks."

"No problem," he said.

"He was supposed to meet me at the doors," I said. "You see a guy named, uh…" I checked the receipt that was taped to the box. "Irwin Pounder?"

"Pounder, hah," the kid said. "He'll be in his room. Fourth floor, south hall, third door on the left. Just listen for the noise."

"Music?"

He tittered. "Not exactly."

I thanked him and ambled up the stairs, which were getting to be a lot harder on my knees than they used to be. Maybe I needed orthopedic shoes or something.

I got to the second floor before I felt it. There was a tension in the air, something that made my heart speed up and my skin feel hot. A few steps farther, and I started breathing faster and louder. It wasn't until I got to the third floor that I remembered that the most dangerous aspect of a psychic assault is that the victim almost never realizes that it's actually happening.

I stopped and threw up my mental defenses in a sudden panic, and the surge of adrenaline and fear suddenly overcame the tremors of restless need that I'd been feeling. The air was thick with psychic power of a nature I'd experienced once before, back in the Raith Deeps. That was when Lara Raith had unleashed the full force of her come hither against her own father, the White King, drowning his mind in imposed lust and desire to please her. He'd been her puppet ever since.

This was the same form of attack, though there were subtle differences. It had to be Barrowill. He'd moved even faster than I'd feared. I kept my mental shields up as I picked up my pace. By the time I reached the fourth floor, I heard the noise the amiable toker had mentioned.

It was sex. Loud sex. A lot of it.

I dropped the pizza and drew my blasting rod. It took me about five seconds to realize what was happening. Barrowill must have been pushing Connie, psychically—forcing her to continue feeding and feeding after she would normally have stopped. He wanted her to kill Irwin like a good little vampire, and the overflow was spilling out onto the entire building.

Not that it takes much to make college kids interested in sex, but in this instance, they had literally gone wild. When I looked down the four hallways, doors were standing wide open. Couples and...well, the only word that really applied was *clusters* of kids were in the act, some of them right out in the hall. Imagine an act of lust. It was going on in at least two of those four hallways.

I turned down Irwin's hall, channeling my will into my blasting rod—and yes, I'm aware of the Freudian irony, here. The carved runes along its length began to burn with silver and scarlet light as the power built up in it. A White Court vampire is practically a pussycat compared to some of the other breeds on the planet, but I'd once seen one of them twist a pair of fifty-pound steel dumbbells around one another to make a point. I might not have much time to throw down on Barrowill in these narrow quarters, and my best chance was to put him down hard the instant I saw him.

I moved forward as silently as I knew how, stepping around a pair of couples who were breaking some sort of municipal statute, I was sure. Then I leaned back and kicked open the door to Irwin's room.

The place looked like a small tornado had gone through it. Books and clothing and bedclothes and typical dorm room décor had been scattered everywhere. The chair next to a small study desk had been knocked over. A laptop computer lay on its side, showing what I'd once been told was a blue screen of death. The bed had fallen onto its side, where two of the legs appeared to have snapped off.

Connie and Irwin were there, and the haze of lust rolling off the ingénue succubus was a second psychic cyclone. I barely managed to push away. Irwin had her pinned against the wall in a corner. His muscles strained against his skin, and his breath came in dry, labored gasps, but he never stopped moving.

He wasn't being gentle, and Connie apparently didn't mind. Her eyes were a shade of silver, metallic silver, as if they'd been made of chrome, reflecting the room around her like tiny, warped mirrors. She'd sunk her fingers into the drywall to the second knuckle on either side of her to hang on, and her body was rolling in a strained arch in time with his motion. They were gratuitously enthusiastic about the whole thing.

And I hadn't gotten laid in forever.

"Irwin!" I shouted.

Shockingly, I didn't capture his attention.

"Connie!"

I didn't capture hers, either.

I couldn't let the...the, uh, process continue. I had no idea how long it might take, or how resistant to harm Irwin might be, but it would be stupid to do nothing and hope for the best. While I was trying to figure out how to break it up before someone lost an eye, I heard the door of the room across the hall open behind me. The sights and sounds and the haze of psychic influence had my mental processes running at less than peak performance. I didn't process the sound into a threat until Barrowill slugged me on the back of the head with something that felt like a lump of solid ivory.

I don't even remember hitting the floor.

When I woke up, I had a Sasquatch-sized headache, my wrists and ankles were killing me. Half a dozen of Barrowill's goons were all literally kneeling on me to hold me down. Every single one of them had a knife pressed close to one of my major arteries.

Also, my pants had shrunk by several sizes.

I was still in Irwin's dorm room, but things had changed. Irwin was on his back on the floor, Connie astride him. Her features had changed, shifted subtly. Her skin seemed to glow with pale light. Her eyes were empty white spheres. Her cheekbones stood out more harshly against her face, and her hair was a sweat-dampened, wild mane that clung to her cheeks and her parted lips. She was moving as if in slow motion, her fingernails digging into Irwin's chest.

Barrowill's psychic assault was still under way, and Connie's presence had become something so vibrant and penetrating that

for a second I thought there might have been a minor earthquake going on. I had to get to that girl. I *had* to. If I didn't, I was going to lose my mind with need. My instant reaction upon opening my eyes was to struggle to get closer to her on pure reflex.

The goons held me down, and I screamed in protest—but at least being a captive had kept me from doing something stupid and gave me an instant's cold realization that my shields were down. I threw them up again as hard as I could, but the Barrowills had been in my head too long. I barely managed to grab hold of my reason.

The kid looked awful. His eyes were glazed. He wasn't moving with Connie so much as his body was randomly shaking in independent spasms. His head lolled from one side to the other, and his mouth was open. A strand of drool ran from his mouth to the floor.

Barrowill had righted the fallen chair. He sat upon it with one ankle resting on his other knee, his arms folded. His expression was detached, clinical, as he watched his daughter killing the young man she loved.

"Barrowill," I said. My voice came out hoarse and rough. "Stop this."

The vampire directed his gaze to me and shook his head. "It's after midnight, Dresden. It's time for Cinderella to return to her real life."

"You son of a bitch," I snarled. "She's killing him."

A small smile touched one corner of his mouth. "Yes. Beautifully. Her Hunger is quite strong." He made a vague gesture with one hand. "Does he seem upset about it? He's a mortal. And mortals are all born to die. The only question is how and in how much pain."

"There's this life thing that happens in between," I snarled.

"And many more where his came from." Barrowill's eyes went chill. "His. And yours."

"What do you mean?"

"When she's finished, we leave. You're dessert."

A lump of ice settled in my stomach, and I swallowed. All things considered, I was becoming a little worried about the outcome of this situation. *Talk, Harry. Keep him talking. You've never met a vampire who didn't love the sound of his own voice. Something could change the situation if you play for time.*

"Why not do it before I woke up?" I asked.

"This way is more efficient," Barrowill said. "If a young athlete takes Ecstasy, and his heart fails, there may be a candlelight vigil, but there won't be an investigation. Two dead men? One of them a private investigator? There will be questions." He shrugged a shoulder. "And I don't care for you to bequest me your death curse, wizard. But once Connie has you, you won't have enough left of your mind to speak your own name, much less utter a curse."

"The Raiths are going to kill you if you drag the Court and the Council into direct opposition," I said.

"The Raiths will never know. I own twenty ghouls, Dresden, and they're always hungry. What they leave of your corpse won't fill a moist sponge."

Connie suddenly ceased moving altogether. Her skin had become pure ivory white. She shuddered, her breaths coming in ragged gasps. She tilted her head back and a low, throaty moan came out of her throat. I've had sex that wasn't as good as Connie sounded.

Dammit, Dresden. Focus.

I was out of time.

"The Council will find out, Chuck. They're *wizards*. Finding unfindable information is what they *do*."

He smirked. "I think we both know that their reputation is very well constructed."

We *did* both know that. Dammit. "You think nobody's going to miss me?" I asked. "I have friends, you know."

Barrowill suddenly leaned forward, focusing on Connie, his eyes becoming a few shades lighter. "Perhaps, Dresden. But your friends are not here."

Then there was a crash so loud that it shook the building. Barrowill's sleek, black Lincoln Town Car came crashing through the dorm room's door, taking a sizable portion of the wall with it. The ghouls holding me down were scattered by the debris, and fine dust filled the air.

I started coughing at once, but I could see what had happened. The car had come through from the far side of this wing of the dorm, smashing through the room where Barrowill had waited in ambush. The car had crossed the hall and wound up with its bumper and front tires resting inside Irwin's room. It had smashed a massive hole in the outer brick wall of the building, leaving it gaping open to the night.

That got everyone's attention. For an instant, the room was perfectly silent and perfectly still. The ghoul chauffeur still sat in the driver's seat—only his head wobbled loosely, leaning at a right angle to the rest of his neck.

"Hah," I cackled, wheezing. "Hah, hah. Heh hah, hah, hah. Moron."

A large figure leapt up to the hole in the exterior wall and landed in the room across the hall, hitting with a crunch only slightly less massive than the car had made. I swear to you, if I'd heard that sound effect they used to use when Steve Austin jumped somewhere, I would not have been shocked. The other room was unlit, and the newcomer was a massive, threatening shadow.

He slapped a hand the size of a big cookie tray on the floor and let out a low, rumbling sound like nothing I'd ever heard this side of an amplified bass guitar. It was music. You couldn't have written it in musical notation, any more than you could write the music of a thunderstorm, or write lyrics to the song of a running stream. But it was music nonetheless.

Power like nothing I had ever encountered surged out from that impact, a deep, shuddering wave that passed visibly through the dust in the air. The ceiling and the walls and the floor sang in resonance with the note and impact alike, and Barrowill's psychic assault was swept away like a sand castle before the tide. Connie's eyes flooded with color, changing from pure, empty whiteness back to a rich blue as deep and rich as a glacial lake, and the humanity came flooding back into her features. The sense of wild panic in the air suddenly vanished, and for another timeless instant, everything, *everything* in that night went utterly silent and still.

Holy.

Crap.

I've worked with magic for decades, and take it from me, it really isn't very different from anything else in life. When you work with magic, you rapidly realize that it is far easier to disrupt than to create, far more difficult to mend than to destroy. Throw a stone into a glass-smooth lake, and ripples will wash over the whole thing. Making waves with magic instead of a rock would have been easy.

But if you can make that lake smooth again—that's one hell of a trick.

That surge of energy didn't attack anything or anybody. It didn't destroy Barrowill's assault.

It made the water smooth again.

Strength of a River in His Shoulders opened his eyes, and his fury made them burn like coals in the shadows—but he simply crouched, doing nothing.

All of Barrowill's goons remained still, wide eyes flicking from River to Barrowill and back.

"Back off, Chuck," I said. "He's giving you a chance to walk away. Take him up on it."

The vampire's expression was completely blank as he stood among the debris. He stared at River Shoulders for maybe three seconds—and then I saw movement behind River Shoulders.

Clawed hands began to grip the edges of the hole behind River. Wicked, bulging red eyes appeared. Monstrous-looking *things* in the same general shape as a human appeared in complete silence.

Ghouls.

Barrowill didn't have six goons with him.

He'd brought them *all*.

Barrowill spat toward River, bared his teeth and screamed, "Kill it!"

And it was on.

Everything went completely insane. The human-shaped ghouls in the room bounded forward, their faces and limbs contorting, tearing their way out of their cheap suits as they assumed their true forms. More ghouls poured in through the hole in the wall like a swarm of panicked roaches. I couldn't get an accurate count of the enemy—the action was too fast. But twenty sounded about right. Twenty flesh-rending, superhumanly strong and durable predators flung themselves onto River Shoulders in an overwhelming wave. He vanished beneath a couple of *tons* of hungry ghoul. It was *not* a fair fight.

Barrowill should have brought more goons.

There was an enormous bellow, a sound that could only have been made by a truly massive set of lungs, and ghouls exploded outward from River Shoulders like so much hideous shrapnel. Several were flung back out of the building. Others

slammed into walls with so much force that they shattered the drywall. One of them went *through* the ceiling, then fell limply back down into the room—only to be caught by the neck in one of River Shoulders's massive hands. He squeezed, crushing the ghoul's neck like soft clay, and there was an audible pop. The ghoul spasmed once, then River flung the corpse into the nearest batch of monsters.

After that, it was clobbering time.

Barrowill moved fast, seizing Connie and darting out the door. I looked around frantically and spotted one of the knives the goons had been holding before they transformed. My hands and ankles had been bound in those plastic restraining strips, and I could barely feel my fingers, but I managed to pick up the knife and cut my legs free. Then I put it on the front bumper of the Lincoln, stepped on it with one foot to hold it in place, and after a few moments managed to cut my hands loose as well.

The dorm sounded like a medley of pay-per-view wrestling and the *Island of Doctor Moreau*. Ghouls shrieked. River Shoulders roared. Very, very disoriented students screamed. The walls and floor shook with impact again and again as River Shoulders flung ghouls around like so many softballs. Ghoulish blood spattered the walls and the ceiling, green-brown and putrid-smelling, and as strong as he was, River Shoulders wasn't pitching a shutout. The ghouls' claws and fangs had sunk into him, covering him in punctures and lacerations, and his scarlet blood mixed with theirs on the various surfaces.

I tried to think unobtrusive thoughts, stayed low, and went to Irwin. He still looked awful, but he was breathing hard and steady, and he'd already begun blinking and trying to focus his eyes.

"Irwin!" I shouted. "Irwin! Where's her purse?"

"Whuzza?" Irwin mumbled.

"Connie's purse! I've got to help Connie! Where is her purse?"

Irwin's eyes almost focused. "Connie?"

"Oh never *mind*." I started ransacking the dorm room until I found Connie's handbag. She had a brush in it. The brush was liberally festooned with her blond hairs.

I swept a circle into the dust on the floor, tied the hair around my pentacle amulet and invested the circle with a whisper of will. Then I quickly worked the tracking spell that was generally my bread and butter when I was doing investigator stuff. When I released the magic, it rushed down into Connie's borrowed hair, and my amulet lurched sharply out of plumb and held itself steady at a thirty- or forty-degree angle. Connie went thataway.

I ducked a flying ghoul, leapt over a dying ghoul, and staggered down the hall at my best speed while the blood went back into my feet.

I had gone down one whole flight of stairs without falling when the angle on the amulet changed again. Barrowill had gone down one floor, then taken off down one of the residential hallways toward the fire escape at the far end. He'd bypassed security by ripping the door off its hinges, then flinging it into the opposite wall. Kids were scattering out of the hallway, looking either horrified or disappointed. Some both. Barrowill had reached the far end, carrying his daughter over one shoulder, and was headed for the fire door.

Barrowill had been savvy enough to divest me of my accoutrements, but I was still a wizard, dammit, blasting rod or no. I drew up my will, aimed low, and snarled, *"Forzare!"*

Pure kinetic force lashed invisibly through the air and caught Barrowill at the ankles. It kicked both of his feet up into the air, and he took a pratfall onto the floor. Connie landed with a grunt and bounced to one side. She lay there dazed and blinking.

Barrowill slithered back up to his feet, spinning toward me, and producing a pistol in one hand. I lurched back out of the line of fire as the gun barked twice, and bullets went by me with a double hiss. I went to my knees and bobbed my head out into the hall again for a quick peek, jerking it back immediately. Barrowill was picking Connie up. His bullet went through the air where my head would have been if I'd been standing.

"Don't be a moron, Harry," I said. "You came for the kid. He's safe. That's all you were obligated to do. Let it g—oh who am I kidding. There's a girl."

I didn't have to beat the vampire—I just had to slow him down long enough for River Shoulders to catch up to him... assuming River *did* pursue.

I took note of which wing Barrowill was fleeing through and rushed down the stairs to the ground floor. Then I left the building and sprinted to the far end of that wing.

Barrowill slammed the emergency exit open and emerged from the building. He was moving fast, but he also had his daughter to carry, and she'd begun to resist him, kicking and thrashing, slowing him down. She tugged him off balance just as he shot at me again, and it went wide. I slashed at him with another surge of force, but this time I wasn't aiming for his feet—I went for the gun. The weapon leapt out of his hands and went spinning away, shattering against the bricks of the dorm's outer wall. Another blast knocked Connie off his shoulder, and she let out a little shriek. Barrowill staggered, then let out a snarl of frustration and charged me at a speed worthy of the Flash's understudy.

I flung more force at him, but Barrowill bobbed to one side, evading the blast. I threw myself away from the vampire and managed to roll with the punch he sent at my head. He caught me an inch or two over one eyebrow, the hardest and most impact-resistant portion of the human skull. That and the fact that I'd managed to rob it of a little of its power meant that he only sent me spinning wildly away, my vision completely obscured by pain and little silver stars. He was furious, his power rolling over me like a sudden deluge of ice water, to the point where crystals of frost formed on my clothing.

Barrowill followed up, his eyes murderous—and then Bigfoot Irwin bellowed, "Connie!" and slammed into Barrowill at the hip, using his body as a living spear. Barrowill was flung to one side, and Irwin pressed his advantage, still screaming, coming down atop the vampire and pounding him with both fists in elemental violence, his sunken eyes mad with rage. "Connie! Connie!"

I tried to rise but couldn't seem to make it past one knee. So all I could do was watch as the furious scion of River Shoulders unleashed everything he had on a ranking noble of the White Court. Barrowill could have been much stronger than a human being if he'd had the gas in the tank—but he'd spent his energy on his psychic assault, and it had drained him. He still thrashed powerfully, but he was no match for the enraged young man. Irwin slammed Barrowill's nose flat against his face. I saw one of the vampire's teeth go flying into the night air. Slightly-too-pale blood began to splash against Irwin's fists.

Christ. If the kid killed Barrowill, the White Court would consider it an act of war. All kinds of horrible things could unfold. "Irwin!" I shouted. "Irwin, stop!"

Kid Bigfoot didn't listen to me.

I lurched closer to him but only made it about six inches before my head whirled so badly that I fell onto my side. "Irwin, stop!" I looked around and saw Connie staring dazedly at the struggle. "Connie!" I said. "Stop him! Stop him!"

Meanwhile, Irwin had beaten Barrowill to within an inch of his life—and now he raised his joined hands over his head, preparing for a sledgehammer blow to Barrowill's skull.

A small, pretty hand touched his wrist.

"Irwin," Connie said gently. "Irwin, no."

"He tried," Irwin panted. "Tried. Hurt you."

"This isn't the way," Connie said.

"Bad man," Irwin growled.

"But you *aren't*," Connie said, her voice very soft. "Irwin. He's still my daddy."

Connie couldn't have physically stopped Irwin—but she didn't need to. The kid blinked several times, then looked at her. He slowly lowered his hands, and Connie leaned down to kiss his forehead gently. "Shhhh," she said. "Shhhh. I'm still here. It's over, baby. It's over."

"Connie," Irwin said, and leaned against her.

I let out a huge sigh of relief and sank back onto the ground. My head hurt.

Officer Dean stared at me for a while. He chewed on a toothpick and squinted at me. "Got some holes."

"Yeah?" I asked. "Like what?"

"Like all those kids saw a Bigfoot and them whatchamacalits. Ghouls. How come they didn't say anything?"

"You walked in on them while they were all still trying to put their clothes back on. After flinging themselves into random sex with whoever happened to be close to them. They're all denying that this ever happened right now."

"Hngh," Dean said. "What about the ghoul corpses?"

"After Irwin dragged their boss up to the fight, the ghouls quit when they saw him. River Shoulders told them all to get out of his sight and take their dead with them. They did."

Dean squinted and consulted a list. "Pounder is gone. So is Connie Barrowill. Not officially missing, or nothing. Not yet. But where are they?"

I looked at Dean and shrugged.

I'd seen ghouls in all kinds of situations before—but I'd never seen them whipped into submission. Ghouls fought to the grisly, messy end. That was what they did. But River Shoulders had been more than their match. He'd left several of them alive when he could have killed them to the last, and he'd found their breaking point when Irwin had dragged Barrowill in by his hair. Ghouls could take a huge beating, but River Shoulders had given them one like I'd never seen, and when he ordered them to take their master and their dead and never to return, they'd snapped to it.

"Thanks, Connie," I groaned as she settled me onto a section of convenient rubble. I was freezing. The frost on my clothes was rapidly melting away, but the chill had settled inward.

The girl looked acutely embarrassed, but that wasn't in short supply in that dorm. That hallway was empty of other students for the moment, though. We had the place to ourselves, though I judged that the authorities would arrive in some form before long.

Irwin came over with a dust-covered blanket and wrapped it around her. He'd scrounged a ragged towel for himself though it did more to emphasize his physique than to hide it. The kid was ripped.

"Thank you, Irwin," she said.

He grunted. Physically, he'd bounced back from the nearly lethal feeding like a rubber freaking ball. Maybe River Shoulders's water-smoothing spell had done something to help that. Mentally, he was slowly refocusing. You could see the gleam coming back into his eyes. Until that happened, he'd listened to Connie. A guy could do worse.

"I..." Connie shook her head. "I remember all of it. But I have no idea what just happened." She stared at River Shoulders for a moment, her expression more curious than fearful. "You... You stopped something bad from happening, I think."

"Yeah, he did," I confirmed.

Connie nodded toward him in a grateful little motion. "Thank you. Who are you?"

"Irwin's dad," I said.

Irwin blinked several times. He stared blankly at River Shoulders.

"Hello," River rumbled. How something that large and that powerful could sit there bleeding from dozens of wounds and somehow look sheepish was beyond me. "I am very sorry we had to meet like that. I had hoped for something quieter. Maybe with music. And good food."

"You can't stay," I said to River. "The authorities are on the way."

River made a rumbling sound of agreement. "This is a disaster. What I did..." He shook his head. "This was in such awful taste."

"Couldn't have happened to nicer guys, though," I said.

"Wait," Connie said. "Wait. What the *hell* just happened here?"

Irwin put a hand on her shoulder, and said, to me, "She's... she's a vampire. Isn't she?"

I blinked and nodded at him. "How did...?"

"Paranet," he said. "There's a whole page."

"Wait," Connie said again. "A...what? Am I going to sparkle or something?"

"God, no," said Irwin and I, together.

"Connie," I said, and she looked at me. "You're still exactly who you were this morning. And so is Irwin. And that's what counts. But right now, things are going to get really complicated if the cops walk in and start asking you questions. Better if they just never knew you were here."

"This is all so…" She shook her head. Then she stared at River Shoulders. Then at me. "Who *are* you?"

I pointed at me, and said, "Wizard." I pointed at River. "Bigfoot." I pointed at Irwin. "Son of Bigfoot." I pointed at her. "Vampire. Seriously."

"Oh," she said faintly.

"I'll explain it," Irwin told her quietly. He was watching River Shoulders.

River held out his huge hands to either side and shrugged. "Hello, son."

Irwin shook his head slowly. "I…never really…" He sucked in a deep breath, squared off against his father, and said, "Why?"

And there it was. What had to be the Big Question of Irwin's life.

"My people," he said. "Tradition is very important to them. If I acknowledged you…they would have insisted that certain traditions be observed. It would have consumed your life. And I didn't want that for you. I didn't want that for your mother. I wanted your world to be wider than mine."

Bigfoot Irwin was silent for a long moment. Then he scratched at his head with one hand and shrugged. "Tonight…really explains a lot." He nodded slowly. "Okay. We aren't done talking. But okay."

"Let's get you out of here," River said. "Get you both taken care of. Answer all your questions."

"What about Harry?" Irwin said.

I couldn't get any more involved with the evident abduction of a scion of the White Court. River's mercy had probably kept the situation from going completely to hell, but I wasn't going to drag the White Council's baggage into the situation. "You guys go on," I told them. "I do this kind of thing all the time. I'll be fine."

"Wow, seriously?" Irwin asked.

"Yeah," I said. "I've been in messier situations than this. And...it's probably better if Connie's dad has time to cool off before you guys talk again. River Shoulders can make sure you have that time."

Outside, a cart with flashing bulbs on it had pulled up.

"River," I said. "Time's up."

River Shoulders rose and nodded deeply to me. "I'm sorry that I interfered. It seemed necessary."

"I'm willing to overlook it," I said. "All things considered."

His face twisted into a very human-looking smile, and he extended his hand to Irwin. "Son."

Irwin took his father's hand, one arm still around Connie, and the three of them didn't vanish so much as...just become less and less relevant to the situation. It happened over the course of two or three seconds, as that same nebulous, somehow transparent power that River had used earlier enfolded them. And then they were all gone.

Boots crunched down the hall, and a uniformed officer with a name tag reading DEAN burst in, one hand on his gun.

Dean eyed me, then said, "That's all you know, huh?"

"That's the truth," I said. "I told you that you wouldn't believe it. You gonna let me go now?"

"Oh, hell no," Dean said. "That's the craziest thing I've ever heard. You're stoned out of your mind or insane. Either way, I'm going to put you in the drunk tank until you have a chance to sleep it off."

"You got any aspirin?" I asked.

"Sure," he said, and got up to get it.

My head ached horribly, and I was pretty sure I hadn't heard the end of this, but I was clear for now. "Next time, Dresden," I muttered to myself, "just take the gold."

Then Officer Dean put me in a nice quiet cell with a nice quiet cot, and there I stayed until Wild Bill Meyers showed up the next morning and bailed me out.